Short Stories II

by Gene Bushey

DORRANCE PUBLISHING CO
EST. 1920
PITTSBURGH, PENNSYLVANIA 15238

Dorrance Publishing Co
585 Alpha Drive
Suite 103
Pittsburgh, PA 15238
Visit our website at *www.dorrancebookstore.com*

ISBN: 979-8-88729-387-5
eISBN: 979-8-88729-887-0

Absorb

It all started in the middle of Kansas. A boy named Tommy Burns was playing outside when he saw this small object fall from the sky. He quickly ran over to where it landed to take a closer look. As he crouched down, he noticed the small, sphere-shaped ball glistening in the grass and knew that it must have been the object that fell from the sky. Without thinking, Tommy reached down and scooped the ball up into his hands, with immediate regret.

"OUCH!" Tommy screamed at the top of his lungs as the ball sent electrical pins and needles all throughout his frozen body. He couldn't move and was locked in place as the ball continued to whirl inside his body.

As the current started to slow its movement through Tommy, his knees began to shake uncontrollably. His eyes sprang open and just as fast as they had opened, his body collapsed to the ground, and his conscientiousness left.

"Tommy! It's time to come inside. Where are you?" Tommy could faintly hear the echo of his mother's voice within his head and tried with all his might to open his eyes. As they fluttered open, Tommy slowly sat up and got to his feet.

"I guess I should get home, then." He took one step, and in a blink, he was at the bottom step of the stairs to his home.

"What?" Tommy glanced around and was amazed at how fast he got back to his house. He thought to himself that it would have taken a few minutes to walk home, but it felt like he just appeared. He shook that thought away and made his way into the house.

"Are you hungry, dear? I made us some sandwiches if you want one." Tommy's mother set the table up as he nodded in agreement to some sandwiches.

"I think I'm going to go for a bike ride after I eat, is that okay, Mom?"

"Of course, just make sure to keep your helmet on, and no later than dusk are you to be home." Tommy scarfed down his food, gave a quick hug to his mother, and headed back out into the stiff Kansas summer air.

Tommy hopped on his bike and thought of riding down to the pond, which is a nice ten- to fifteen-minute ride away. Just as he looked down to place his foot on the pedal, he glanced up and was met with the view of the pond he just thought about seconds ago.

"What the heck!" Tommy gasped and jumped off his bike in horror. He sits on the grass near the edge of the pond, shaking and wondering what was going on.

"I was just at home. This can't be possible, can it?" Tommy started to pace and think about what had happened earlier this morning with the ball that fell from the sky.

"It couldn't be!" Tommy begins to think of another location to prove if what he believes is happening, is actually happening. He closed his eyes, and when he opened them back up seconds later, he is face to face with the barn on the opposite side of his house.

"HAHA! This is incredible!" Tommy starts laughing hysterically imagining all of the places he can be with just a thought.

He runs over to the front side of the house where a huge tree sits in the front lawn, a tree he's tried to climb to the top before but could never make it. At the base of the tree, with one thought and a set of closed eyes, Tommy imagines he's at the top of the tree, gazing across the open fields that surround his home. He opens his eyes and takes in the view he only dreamed he'd be able to see. As calm as the view is, Tommy hears a creak from the branch he is perched on, and his heart skips a beat. As he closes his eyes to leave the tree, he feels the sudden movement, and when they open back up, he's underneath his bed in the house.

Tommy can't help but laugh at where he landed this time, but knew that he would have to work on controlling whatever this was. As he crawled out from under the bed, he felt dizzy and weak, and knew he shouldn't play around with whatever this was too much.

Tommy decides to go back to the barn and field where he saw the ball fall out of the sky, and with all the control he can muster, he walks all the way to the barn.

He decides to walk around and see if the ball is somewhere hiding in the grass, when he stops dead in his tracks from a voice he hears coming from the sky.

"Tommy. You are the one we will use for our studies. You have been warned." Tommy shakes his head in disbelief and continues looking for the ball.

"As if. I must be hearing things now." For the rest of the day Tommy doesn't use this weird power he has and doesn't think twice about the voice he heard while looking for the ball. As nightfall comes, Tommy tries his hardest to guide himself to stay thinking about his bed, but as his dreams go, he sleeps deeper and deeper, and next thing he realizes is he's at the pond's edge again because of the dream he was having with his friends. One quick thought and he's back in his bed safe and sound.

As Tommy drifts deeper into sleep again, he then has a dream, but it's one that he never has had before. He's standing in front of this board of people who he has never seen before. They explain things to him about what happened to him and what he's supposed to do for them. He then understood what the sphere was sent on the planet for: research and to see if they could live among us.

As time went on, He would have a lot of fun moving back and forth from place to place to try and fool my mom and friends, it was a lot of fun to do, but then one night he was woken up by this buzzing in his head. It kind of hurt. He was wondering, *What's going on?* He then would hear this voice, come out to the pond: "We need to talk." So he went to the pond, and he's there, and there are people there with him as he is wondering what's going on. Just then, one man moves forward and is talking to me with our minds. We never move our mouths, and I just think, *That's amazing.* He asked me how I was doing with this gift they have given me, and I tell him, "I'm doing great. No one has found out how I have been doing this for years, and now at the age of eighteen, I'm really finding out other things I have, like this here, where I can talk without moving my mouth."

The man then told me on my twentieth birthday, "You will be ready for us."

I was like, "What do you mean ready for you?"

He then said, "You will be coming with us. All the things that you absorbed and thoughts you learned, we are going to bring you back with us so we can study you. It's what happens to you when the sphere choses you. You have no say. If you stay here, you will die; it's just what happens. Do you remember the dust from the sphere? That's what's going to happen to you if you don't come with us."

He was so scared; he didn't want to leave this place. His family and his friends are here. "There must be another way," he said to the people.

They said, "Nope, this is the only way."

He then said, "I'll go now, then bring me back."

They said, "No, it doesn't work like that. We are sorry."

He wakes up from that and says, "There is something wrong. I'm not going. There has to be something I can do." So, that afternoon, he went through all the stuff he absorbed and went over and over trying to figure out what he has learned, and then he tried to forget it all. Maybe they will figure out that he's not so valuable to them. So he went to all the places that he learned and absorbed about and all the people he met, doing as much forgetting as he could, hoping it was enough that they wouldn't be interested in him. Days went by, and he was trying his hardest to forget. It was working, but he was running out of time.

That night, they contacted him and said, "Be ready tomorrow."

He started to panic. "I don't want to go with them. I'm too young. somebody help me!" Just like that, he is frozen in his tracks.

The people ask him, "Why do you refuse to learn and not absorb?"

He said, "I don't want to leave my family and my friends and earth. I love it here."

They then say, "We don't compute that, and we don't understand."

I told them, "This is what we do here on Earth; it's not about collecting things, it's about living the moment, not absorbing everything, and then dissection."

That's not going to help you to understand". So, they released him, and then next thing he knew his hand is flat and the sphere is coming out of him and forming itself into the ball like it was when he found it. Just then, he hears the man talk to him, and he says, "I will never understand your kind. You would have done anything to stay here."

"Yes, I would have. It's our culture; maybe you should see how we live first before you have someone absorb everything, instead of seeing how people live."

The End

Bullied

It all started on my twelfth birthday. My dad bought me a Schwinn bike, and man, was it sweet. Not only was it a bright yellow with white strips; it also had a huge banana seat and a stick shift. YES, a stick shift. It was a one-of-a-kind bike, and all the kids in my neighborhood wanted one, but they were so expensive. My older cousin gave it to my dad to give to me for my birthday, as he had outgrown it and didn't ride it any longer. For the longest time I rode that bike everywhere: to the store down the road, off to visit Gram's, even sometimes to school if I was lucky. But with such a sweet ride, I knew it would be a matter of time before the kids in my area started to say stuff.

Jealousy started to squeeze into every conversation and passing with the kids in my housing development.

"Why would a cheewee like you have such a nice bike? You don't deserve it!" Names and insults thrown every time I left the house on my bike. Everyone wanted my bike, but I knew I deserved it; it was the greatest gift I've ever gotten. I was a bigger kid back then, so a lot of the older kids would leave me alone because of my size, but they wouldn't hold back from the jokes and picking. That bike was one of the highlights of my childhood, and I loved that everyone wanted what I had.

Thinking back on it now, I was just about ready to graduate from the police academy and move into a home I bought down the street from my mom and dad's when I saw the bike again. They were wondering when I was going to go through all of my stored stuff in the garage, and when the day came that

I finally did it, I couldn't believe my eyes. Nestled in the back, covered from the dust and loose items, was my bright yellow bike in perfect mint condition. I made my way out of the garage with my bike and called my parents out to take a look.

"I think it's time to give this bike to another kid who will love it as much as I did." My parents nodded and smiled at the idea.

"I still remember how excited you were when you first got that bike. You rode it everywhere," my mom exclaimed with a bright smile.

"I was just glad to see you exploring on your own. I know you loved that bike more than anything else," my dad said with his hand on my shoulder.

"There is a kid down the street named Timmy," my mom detailed. "I work with his mother. They don't have much, and I would imagine it would make him feel on top of the world with a bike like that."

"That's a great idea. I'll clean it up and pump air into the tires, and it will be good to go!"

I decided to ride the bike over to Timmy's because I couldn't give it away without one final goodbye ride. Kids in yards the entire way to Timmy's were staring as I rode down the road, whispering to each other about the bike. It felt great to see their faces, and I couldn't wait to see Timmy's when he gets to take his first ride on it.

Once I got to Timmy's house and knocked on the door, his mother answered the door.

"Hi, my mom Rita sent me over." I introduced myself and told her what I was going to do for Timmy.

"What a fantastic idea! He will be so happy!" She was so happy for him and had tears in her eyes. "He has such a hard time in school, always getting bullied and picked on."

"I get that. I feel for him. School wasn't the easiest for me when I was his age, either." I nod my head but feel bad for Timmy.

"He will be back tomorrow. He's with his dad for the night. You could place it in the garage for him to find when he gets home. Thank you again. You're going to make him the happiest boy on the block!" She reached out to hug me and waved as I walked the bike to their garage.

I left their house feeling as good as I could. As I walked down pass the houses, I noticed some of the kids looking and noticing I didn't have the bike, and they must have put two and two together, but I didn't care. Timmy needed a bike, and he's a good kid. I felt good for giving him a gift he'll enjoy for years to come, something he can feel good about when others are putting him down.

A few days went by and while at work, I started to get worried that Timmy wasn't ever going to get me that thank you, but I couldn't imagine why. I thought back and forth if I saw him on the bike, or even around the neighborhood, but had a feeling something was just not right. I asked my mom for Timmy's mom's phone number, so I could check in with his mother and make sure everything was all right with him.

"Thank you for calling. Really. It means so much. I haven't seen Timmy in hours, and he is usually so good at keeping in touch with me if he is going to be late. You haven't seen him, have you? He said he was going to ride up to your house today to say thank you for the bike." I could hear the panic in her voice, and I felt shivers go down my back.

"I'm sorry. I haven't seen Timmy at all. He hasn't ridden up to my house, my parents have been there all day and no one has visited. Let me ask around and we can go from there, okay?" I was trying to be as calm as I could, but I couldn't shake the feeling of something being off.

She thanked me and hung up. I started to call some of the families on the road to my house from Timmy's, but no one had seen the kid since yesterday morning when he got back from his father's house. I grabbed my jacket and told the police chief I needed to talk with some kids and that something might be wrong, but I would be back at the station in a few hours.

I hurried over to where most of the kids hang out in a park between Timmy's house and mine and asked the kids if they had seen Timmy recently.

"We were playing some game yesterday morning, but no one has seen him since. We would definitely have remembered because everyone has been talking about his new bike." Other kids echoed in and said the same things. I knew it would be good to get some local people together to figure this out, so I thanked the kids and ran over to Timmy's house to speak with his mother in person.

I sat down in her home while she made some coffee. I could tell she was nervous and just wanted answers about her son.

"I've spoken with parents and kids on the street about when they saw Timmy last. Everyone remembers seeing him yesterday morning. Did he come home last night?"

"Oh, he didn't." She was in tears at this point. "I was hoping he would have called if he decided to stay the night at a friend's house. He never just leaves and doesn't come back. I am horrified I didn't contact anyone sooner. Is it too late?" I took her hands in mine.

"Of course not. Let me call the police chief and have you file a missing person's report and why don't you invite some friends over to keep you calm. We'll get a neighborhood search going before it gets too dark and see if we can't find him." She nodded as tears rolled down her eyes, and I excused myself to call the station.

"Police Chief Myers," my boss answered right away.

"Chief Myers, I'm calling with some more information about the boy I left the station to look for. The mother hasn't seen him since yesterday morning and has had no contact from him since then. Neighborhood kids and parents confirm her timeline. She would like to file a missing person's report, and I would like permission to set up a search party for the next few hours before the sun sets."

"Officer Bushey, thank you for the update. You have permission to set up the search party. I'll send over Officer Adams to the woman's home to help her file the report. Keep us posted on next steps." With that he hung up, and I was relieved the conversation went so well. At least this was a bit of good news to share with Timmy's mother.

After knocking on dozens of doors, I had about thirty people ready to split up and search for Timmy before the sun set. Timmy's mother had a few close friends with her as she went through the missing person's report with Officer Adams. For hours we screamed into the backyards and forest paths for Timmy, but no one found anything suspicious. After four hours, we all met back up and called it a night. I thanked the people who offered to help but took notice of the ones that were not there. I knew it would be a long night. I needed to get back to the station and see what Chief Myers wanted us to do next.

"The search party came up with nothing. No bike, no paths, nothing. What do you think our next move should be?" I was anxious to be leading this case as it was only nearly my first month out of the police academy, but it happened on my road. I felt a personal attachment to this case and wanted to be involved in finding Timmy.

"Okay, let's start by requesting interviews with all of the kids in the neighborhood. You call the parents. Make it clear they are allowed to accompany their children in the interview. We just want to get more information and set the timeline straight. That should give us what we need to move further." I nodded my head in response and thanked him for allowing me to be involved.

I spent a few more hours at my desk making phone calls to the families I knew on our street and had nine interviews set for the next day. Close to midnight, I decided to call it quits for the day and head back home. I just hope it would be a more productive day and that we would find Timmy soon.

The next day, there are the nine kids waiting in the lobby of the station, some with worried faces, others not phased at all. One by one we invited them into an interrogation room to ask questions and find some answers. I'm thankful that no parents showed up, it will be easier to find out the information we need.

After eight interviews I'm starting to lose hope. It doesn't seem like any of the kids know what happened or had seen Timmy after he left the park that morning. The last kid, Jeff, enters the room, and we get ready to ask some questions.

"Jeff, could you tell us about the time you last saw Timmy this week?" I notice Jeff's hands are squeezed into fits under the table and his head hangs, avoiding eye contact with anyone in the room.

"I saw him the other day, just like everyone else said, "he mumbled to us.

"Okay, good. Can you tell us anything special about seeing him the other day?" We were hoping to get something out of him before having to be a bit more aggressive.

"Yeah, he had that new bike. Everyone was jealous; he didn't deserve it." We all looked at each other and knew we needed to move forward with caution.

"Jealous? What do you mean? Were there kids who were unhappy at Timmy for getting the bike?" Jeff shook his head and began to mumble more. "Could you repeat that, Jeff? We couldn't quite hear you."

"I just saw something, and I don't know." His hands started to shake a little. "I don't want to get it trouble. I don't even know if it will help."

"Why would you get in trouble, Jeff? We are just trying to help Timmy right now."

"He said he would hurt me if I told anyone." At that we knew Jeff held the information we've been searching for; we just needed to make sure to get it out of him before jumping the gun.

"We can promise you no one will hurt you. No one will know that you gave us any information, and we can make sure to keep it between just us, okay? We just really want to find Timmy and help him as soon as possible, and we think you might have the information we need." Jeff glanced up through the hair laying over his eyes and nodded.

"Okay. I saw Timmy that morning at the park, and I decided to follow him when he left, so maybe I could ride his bike. It was such an awesome bike. I just wanted to take it for a quick spin. I stayed a bit behind him and noticed a kid yelling to him from the porch of this one house. I think it was blue and that kid is homeschooled." We eagerly nodded at Jeff's story; he was definitely giving us the information we needed.

"Yes, that is Dr. Jones's house. Continue," I interjected, so we had more information in our notes.

"I've heard some pretty messed-up stuff about that kid. He likes to hurt things. I've seen him kill stray cats and dogs and drag them into his backyard. I got as close as I could, and I heard him yelling at Timmy about how he didn't deserve that bike, calling him a bunch of mean names. Last I saw was Timmy speed off. I tried to run after him, but the kid on the porch yelled to me too. Told me not to tell anyone about what he said. Before I could respond, he was running into the backyard." Jeff shook his head and lifted his eyes up to look at us. "I don't know if any of this helps, but that kid scared me, and I could tell he scared Timmy, too."

"Jeff, thank you. This helps us so much, and we promise no one will ever find out about what you've told us. It gives us a great starting place, thank you for your time. You're free to go." We all shook hands with him, and Officer Adams gave him a sergeant sticker to make him feel a bit better about what he did. He left with a huge smile and joined his friends for the walk home.

"All right. Bushey and Adams, let's get in the cruiser and get to this Jones's house while we still have light." We nodded in agreement and got into the car with Chief Myers.

When we got to the home, Chief Myers knocked on the door, and we were pleasantly surprised when a woman answered.

"Good afternoon, gentlemen. What can I do for you today?" She smiled at us and waited for our response.

"Good afternoon, Mrs. Jones. We are here to ask for permission to speak with your son. We've have a kid that is missing from the Neiborhood and your son is the last one to have been seen with Timmy. Would you be willing to allow us some time to speak with him at your home?" Her face grew irritated, and we were not ready for her response.

"How dare you assume my Tony has anything to do with the disappearance of this kid! I am calling my husband immediately. Don't come back without a warrant!" She slammed the door in our faces, and we all shook our heads in defeat.

"Well, we still have time today to get a warrant from the judge for tomorrow. How about it, chief?"

"Bushey, that's a great idea. Adams, drop me off at the station and go request a search warrant with Bushey at the courthouse. Take the rest of the day off. We've plenty to look forward to tomorrow." We nodded and headed back to the car.

After getting the warrant request filled by the judge, we went our separate ways for the night, and I dreamt of a sweet reunion for Timmy and his mother, but none of us were aware of what was ahead of us.

The next day, we meet at the Jones's with the warrant to search the property. Chief Myers, Adams, and I walked up to the door to find Dr. Jones lounging in a chair on the porch.

"Good morning, men. I figure you've returned with a warrant?" He doesn't lift an eye from the book he is reading.

"Yes, sir. We have a warrant to search the property and to bring you and your son in for questioning today," the chief stated. With a mere gesture of his hand, Dr. Jones signaled us to enter his home.

The home was incredibly clean and tidy, everything in a specific place and nothing out of the ordinary. We made our way up the stairs to what we could tell was Tony's room. That night we finally convinced the judge to get us a warrant so we could talk to the kid, but the judge wanted Child Services there also, so we go over and get the kid and start looking around the house. Oh boy, the house was very neat, like it was cleaned up, but then we go into the kid's room, and it's dark, goth like, and a lot of pictures of killings, and we all get nervous. We checked the whole room out, and nothing, a lot of pictures of animals killed on Polaroid's, but nothing else. We then notice in the back yard a small shed, and we all get a little excited, and we head out there. We found out that its locked, and it's a huge Master Lock, like an industrial one. We then ask Tony's mom, "Do you have the key to the shed in the back?"

She said, "Oh, that's Tony's shed. He plays in there. He must have it in his room somewhere."

Meanwhile, at the police station, Tony sits with his dad and a person from Child Services. We start by asking him, "Do you know why you are here?"

He said, "No."

We were like, "Have you heard that little Timmy is missing?"

He said, "Really? I haven't heard. I've been outside all day."

I was watching from the two-way mirror, and he never lifted his head. I was pissed because you know he knows something. Then the two detectives leave the room and so did the Child Services personnel; it was just the father and son.

The dad whispered to him, "It's going to be okay."

Tony said, "Are you sure?"

His dad then said, "What did you do?"

He didn't answer.

Just then the Child Service person, named Bob, came in and he said, "Okay, guys. We might have to stop if they push harder."

He said, "But you know he's holding something back."

Bob agreed, but it was too late, and he's a minor, so we were running out of time. We are done with this, when we get back in we are going to asked Tony what does he do in that shed.

He raised his voice and said, "That's my shed. You don't need to go in there."

We said, "Okay, Tony. "

Then Bob stood up and said, "Okay, boys, that's it. We can pick it up tomorrow."

Tony's dad said, "Is he coming home with me?"

"Nope, he's going to the Child Services house until this is over."

We then head over to the shed with bolt cutters and opened the shed. The first thing we find is Timmy's bike, half painted black over the yellow, then we see what looks like a bloody rag in the corner. We take that and are going to see if it's Timmy's blood. I'm sick to my stomach. All of us are. We can't believe it. We search some more and find a bloody hammer and more dried dead animals inside the shed. It's so creepy that a thirteen-year-old boy would have this stuff.

The next day we bring in Tony and he sees his tools, and he noticed them, then starts yelling, "That's my stuff! You didn't have permission to go in there."

One of the officers told him to sit down! He looked at him and said nothing. They then asked Tony, "What happened?"

He didn't say anything, so we left and let Bob talk to him with his dad. Bob started by saying, "Tony, you're in a lot of trouble if you did something to Timmy."

He didn't say a word.

His dad then said, "If you did something, you need to tell the truth."

He then looked at his father and said, "What do you care? You're never there for me, and I hate you." He then had a smile on his face like he was remembering something. At that time, I was so pissed. I wanted to go in there and grab him and say, "HEY, where is Timmy!"

We then get a call.... They found Timmy. Our hearts dropped.

"Where?" said the captain.

"On the bike trail behind the Joneses' house."

The captain then says, "Don't say anything to anyone. We leave it here. After we process the scene, we are going to come back here and get this bastard."

Poor Timmy was stuffed into some bushes and covered up with leaves. It looks like a hit to his head was what caused his death. We were all silent. I never would have thought this would happen around here. I'm in shock. Now the tough part: to go and tell Timmy's mom. As we deliver the bad news, she drops to her knees and said, "Why, why would someone hurt my baby boy!"

I told her as she was in my arms, "I'm going to do whatever I can to get this person." We didn't tell her that we think it's Tony, not sure if she could handle that.

We are driving up to the police station, and I am still trying to process this, but it's tough. I feel like I did this to him because of the bike! I then let that go, and now to nail this monster, because that's what he is. We bring him back in, and we aren't very nice this time. He knows something, so Tony, the officer, slams his hand down and says, "Okay, you little son of bitch, we found Timmy right where you left him, right behind your house. Why did you do it? Come on, I want to know!"

Then Bob was about to say something, and the officer said, "Keep quiet, Bob. This bastard is going to talk!"

Just then Tony picked up his head and said, "I want my lawyer," and smiled at the officer. He almost lost it. We had to get them out of there. I was so shocked; all of us were. It's unreal.

Later that day I get a call from Timmy's mom, and she asked me if the rumors are true about Tony. I said, "Yes, he's been arrested and charged with murdering Timmy." She started to cry and hung the phone up on me.

Later, at the courthouse, after the we got all the jurors and the trial starts, they have to be very easy in using the terms because all the witnesses are young kids. This is going to be tough. As they go through the kids, it starts to get clear that Tony is a bully, and that's what all the kids were saying, and he stole things from people's houses. We are starting to understand that Tony is a real bad kid. They also went on to say that he liked to kill animals and watch them die. They said he took some cats and small dogs and killed them he has issues and needs help. So the prosecutor went on to say that he did what he did because he was jealous of Timmy, and in order to get his bike, he needed to kill him. Just then the Defendant stood up and said, "Your Honer, the prosecutor is speculating."

They went back and looked at each other and said the only way was to put Tony on the stand. He didn't want to, but the judge said, "Okay, everyone out of the room except the court sonographer and the lawyers." So everyone left, the doors were closed, and then the judge said, "Okay, son, come up here and sit down. Remember, you MUST tell the true.

He nodded, and this is how it happened. He started by saying, "That day, Timmy was riding his new bike and riding up to my street with it, rubbing it in that he had a new bike, and he also knew that I wanted that same bike so bad! I went down to the end of the road and told him, 'Get out of here, you spoiled brat,' and he did. That afternoon, I was riding on the bike path and saw Timmy with his bike. I just wanted to ride it, that's all. He said no, so I knocked him off it and said, 'Take mine.' We just traded, and I start to ride it around. Then went down to my shed. I was going to keep it. He comes down with me and says, 'That's my bike.' I told him, 'No, we just traded. Now get out of here,' and then everything went black. The next thing I remember, I have a hammer in my hand, and Timmy is down with a head wound. I drag him up to the bushes and leave him there. All I wanted was the bike, just the BIKE," as Tony starts to yell and cry, and the lawyers just look at each other.

Tony cries some more, and the judge says, "Take him away."

"Where am I going? I didn't mean to do it. What's going to happen to me...? All I wanted was the bike, just the bike."

The End

Calamitous

As I was browsing one day at the local library in the older section at books about murder mysteries, I came across this huge book shoved way in the back of the shelving. It was completely black and about six inches thick, with some eerie looking writing on it. I reached into the shelf to grab it, and as I wiped the line layer of dust off the cover, I spoke the title out loud, "*CALAMITOUS*. What does that mean?"

The book was heavier than it first looked, with a thick leather strap that cut across the front of it fashioned with a large brass buckle. After turning it over in my hands a few times, my eyes stumbled upon a small note tucked in the strap on the front of it that read, "Do Not Undo." I shook my head in confusion, trying to figure out what it meant by undo, and forcing myself not to open it.

I rested the book back on the shelf as I grabbed my phone and started to look up what calamitous meant and why it wouldn't want to be opened. Great misfortune or disaster. *That must be why the warning is on the front*, I thought. Against every better judgement I could think of, my excitement and adrenaline took over my actions, and before I knew it, I was grasping the buckle and undoing the strap. I slowly peeled the cover open and located the first page where I found a welcoming message. With shaky hands and a smile on my face, I began to read what was written.

"Welcome to *Calamitous*, a journey that's going to test every one of your memories. Be prepared for everything, and remember: to leave this book, you must solve the mystery."

To leave this book? What does that even mean? I pondered with worry. My better judgement kicked in, and I tried to close the cover, but it wouldn't budge. It started to shake as a large ball of light engulfed the entire room. I was frozen. I started to feel my body lift off of the floor. It was as if I was shrinking. I looked down and immediately regretted this decision as my feet were slowly sinking into the pages of the book I was holding. I let out a scream, and with that, the front page closed, along with my eyes.

Before I open my eyes, I hear voices of concern surrounding me. I feel a weight leave my shoulders as I realize what happened at the library was all a dream. I smile and begin to flutter my eyes open to the world around me. I first notice that I'm sitting in a chair behind a large desk with packets of papers littered everywhere. I gaze further past the desk with confusion that spread across my face at a group of people are asking if I'm okay, but I'm not me. I'm Detective John Brown.

"Boss, you gotta let us know what is going on in that head of yours. You don't look like yourself." I make eye contact with the man who asks this. I can only imagine he grew up on Staten Island as an Italian American.

"Brown, we got a case to break. What's all this confusion for?" This man spoke with anger and sprayed spit across the room as he chowed down on a donut in the far-right corner of the room.

"Detective. We need you right now. We have to figure out who killed her." This woman spoke with easy and calmness, and with that I struck my first cords with the trio.

"A murder?" I could have asked so many more important questions, but I was intrigued, and I love a good murder mystery.

"Check out the case. Seems to be a boyfriend who murdered his girlfriend at his home of residence. There's all the evidence. We've been trying to find new leads for hours now, and then you decided to doze off right in the middle of it," said the chubbier man, now on to his fourth donut since I woke up.

I picked up the file and started to look at what happened, and it seemed pretty obvious that the boyfriend did the crime, but as I look closer, I start to see things appear on the page. I'm kicked back into reality and remember I'm in a book, and my goal is to figure this crime out. I smile as I realize the book is trying to help me.

"Look at this piece of hair." I motion the Italian American man closer to inspect the hair with me.

"Nothing against you, boss, but I don't know what you want me to look at." He shrugged his shoulders and returned to his cigarette at the left corner of the room.

I shook my head and tried to figure out why no one else can see what I see, and then it clicks. They could be here to distract me, and that would only help the book win versus me winning.

"I'm going to the lab to get this tested again. I think I'm onto something," I detail to the team, and with a few good looks and head nods, I'm out the door and on my way to the lab, but I don't even know the location.

It's as if I already know the way to the lab. I take a few rights and a couple lefts and end up in front of a pair of double doors with the words "DNA Laboratory" printed across the front. I walk into the lab and approach the first person I can find, with my first task weighing heavy on my shoulders.

"I need this hair sample to be tested against the woman who was murdered by her boyfriend. Case file #85117." I receive a nod from the man I approached, and he gives a slight hand motion as I follow him deeper into the lab. I stand off in the corner of the room he has led me into as he runs the hair sample through a multitude of machines. After what feels like an eternity, he prints out a sheet of paper, places the hair back in the bag, and hands both to me.

"Thank you, sir." I reach out my hand for a shake of gratitude, but as my eyes close for a blink, the room starts to spin, and when my eyes reopen, I'm sitting at my desk again with the sheet of paper and hair as if I never left.

"Any luck at the lab, Detective Brown?" I steady my eyes and smile at the three people in front of me.

"We are on the right track, folks. The hair is a match to the victim. Now to dig deeper." I organize my thoughts, and as I go to pick up the file, the book rushes open, and my attention is captured. Two pages glow, with events playing out across the pages as if I'm watching a movie. I realize the two individuals are the boyfriend and girlfriend in the case. I try to capture as many details as I can. The two are arguing, and I'm not able to make out everything they are saying, only what the book wants me to pick up. The boyfriend is complaining that she's hard to live with, an argument they have constantly. But before I can make out anything else, the scene changes, and my breath gets caught in my throat. There is blood everywhere, the scene of the crime where her body is laying limp. I tried to look away, but the book wouldn't let me. There was something I needed to take away from this all. I keep staring at the puddle of blood and I make out an object swimming in the blood, but the book zooms in, and I see it is a necklace. Before I know what's happening, my arm is reaching into the book and grasping the necklace between my fingers. I pull it out of the book and place it in a bag on my desk. The book starts to shake and is closes before I can even look at the scene a second time.

I rush out of my chair with the bag and make my way back to the lab for testing. I go through the steps all over again, flagging down the same man who brings me to the same room with the same machine and the same silence. I shift my weight from foot to foot as the process continues to take minute after minute. I don't realize my eyes are feeling heavy until they shut, and my mind is taken over. I see a scene play out that obviously has to do with the crime. The woman who was murdered is sitting at a nice restaurant with her boyfriend, but before they get their food, they get into an argument and leave the restaurant. I follow them back to the apartment where the crime happened, and I immediately remember this scene from the book. They continue to fight, and he briefly gets physical by pushing her but shakes his head and leaves the scene.

Well, there goes my initial thought on this murder. The book thrusts me back into the present as the lab technician hands me the bag and the piece of paper as I brace myself for the journey back to the office.

But the journey never happened. Instead, I was launched back into a scene, and as I tried to regain my composure, I heard three knocks on a door. As I open my eyes, I'm back inside the woman's apartment as I see her open her door to another woman asking to speak with her. It seems they are friends or at least familiar with each other as the woman seems comfortable around her. She moves out of the way to let her in, and when her back is turned, the woman who just entered smashes her in the back of the head. I gasp and stare, wide-eyed until I'm shaken out of the scene and back into reality.

I'm back at the desk, and my team is eagerly waiting to hear what I've found out, but I need time to process what I just witnessed. I saw the woman who committed the crime, and now all I have to do is figure out who she is and pin her to the crime.

"We need to find the boyfriend and question him immediately. He didn't murder her; it was a friend of hers, and I know exactly what she looks like. Let's get to work." I feel confident in getting this case solved, so the team nods and we get to work.

We invite the boyfriend in for questioning and start to crack away at him to find out who this woman is.

"We need you to identify who this is and what her relationship was with your girlfriend." I shove the detailed drawing to him across the table. I read his composure, and sure enough, he does know her but declines that he does.

"We'll leave you in here to figure out how you know her, and when we get back, we can talk more." He nods in response as we leave the room to strategize more.

"Okay, you've had some time to think about who she is. If we don't get an answer from you then you'll be arrested on conspiracy charges and pinned with the whole crime. We're talking multiple life sentences with no hope for parole. Does that sound like the life you want?" We hope the scare tactic will work with him, and fortunately enough, he is shaking in his boots.

"Okay, okay. She is my other girlfriend." He hangs his head down without looking at us.

"Okay, now what do you think happened to your girlfriend who got murdered and this girlfriend who we have proof of committing that murder?"

"I just think one of them got jealous. I don't know how she even found out. I left that night because we couldn't stop fighting, and I went to the other one's house to check in, and she wasn't there. I promise, I had nothing to do with it." He kept shaking his head as he stared at the table.

"Don't worry, we believe you. We know that she did it, just need to pinpoint her now so we can get a confession." He sighs in relief, and before I can release him, my mind is transported once again into the apartment where the murder happened, and the book must want me to retrace my steps and make sure I'm making the right call here.

I move around the living room and notice the photos on the wall, just of the two of them and no other people. The girlfriend has photos of her and her friends, but none that include the woman who seemed to murder her. I make my way to the trash can that has small bits of paper scattered across the top. I collect the pieces and am transported back into the room with the boyfriend, clutching a small bag of paper pieces.

"Hang tight for a few more hours. We might have a few more questions." He nods in response as I once again make my way to the lab to put the final pieces of the puzzle together.

After seeing the pieces all together, we figure out that it's actually a receipt from a store downtown that sells custom-made masks. Before I know it, I'm walking up to the store with a photo of the boyfriend and the sketch of the woman.

"Did this man enter this store the day before last to purchase a custom-made mask that looked like this woman?" The man studied the photos for what felt like minutes, and eventually nodded in agreement. He left before I could say anything but returned a second later with a bag.

"This guy is the absolute weirdest. He paid the full price for the mask, but said he just wanted to rent it out for a day. He returned it to me not even eight hours after he bought it, and I kept it in this bag until I got around to cleaning it." He shrugged his shoulders, but we had to make sure he didn't clean it yet.

"So, you're saying it hasn't been cleaned yet?" I felt more eager than I should, but he shook his head in response.

"Nope, I. haven't gotten to it yet." I nearly cheer in joy as I find myself walking straight into the forensics lab with the mask in hand, feeling like I'm closer than ever to solving this mystery.

"We need the DNA on this mask as soon as possible with a positive match. We will have his DNA in the system, I know it." I received a nod and patiently waited until they handed me a piece of paper and the bagged mask back.

I'm walking back into the interrogation room while reading the paper with the biggest smile on my face.

"So. Let me walk you through what we've uncovered and then you'll be making your way out of here, how does that sound?" He smiled as if I meant he'd be leaving as a free man. Nope, he'd be leaving in handcuffs to the nearest maximum-security prison.

"You kept getting in arguments with your girlfriend, and of course, I couldn't blame you. It was getting hard to deal with, right?" I received a nod of support, so I continued. "You decide the day before last that you'd go to Masks and More to order a custom-made mask of a woman whom your girlfriend would think is the neighbor, but it was you instead. With a swift blow to the head, she is dead in seconds. You flee the scene, return the mask to the store, and wipe your hands cleans. You come up with a story of a second girlfriend that breaks your case the minute it comes out of your mouth." I take a break to soak in his face; the terror behind his eyes is enough to make me laugh in his face.

"Enjoy your multiple life sentences, sir. It was great speaking with you." He dips his head down and starts to cry as the room is flooding in a bright light. I look out the corner of my eye and see the book opening and my feet shrinking. I've beat the book and solved the mystery.

I shake myself and look around finding myself back at the old library I was in what feels like days ago. I grab my phone off the bookshelf and see only three minutes have passed and release a sigh I didn't realize I was holding in. I pick up the book reclasp it and can't help but smile.

"Goodbye, friend." I place it back in its original home toward the back of the shelf hidden in the shadows of the other books. Closed until the next person decides to open it..

The End

Dark and Dangerous

I guess it all started way back when I was a young man. I heard stories from my grandparents and parents about this eight-foot-tall dark, cloaked man that roams the Sheldon Hill Cemetery. No one has ever gone up there at night. If you do, and you see him, and you will be mesmerized by his stare, and he makes you do strange things until you wake up and you don't remember anything that happened. Dad was telling me that one of his buddies thought he was tough and went up there on a bet, and the next thing, his friends find out that he was stuck in one of the huge maple trees in front. He climbed to the top, like forty feet high, and he doesn't know how he got up there. They had to call the fire department to get him down, and to this day he doesn't drive by that place. He said that the man is real, and he was wrong to think that he wasn't. Dad said he doesn't talk about it to this day; it scared him that much. There have been others that have tried to go up there and have had different experiences. It's a different place at night, and during the day, you hear strange things if you're on one side of the cemetery, then the other. It's just weird. When I was in high school, we heard of a group going up and they never came back until the following night. Rumor has it they went for a hike. No one in the group could recall why they just started walking, but they were found ten miles from the cemetery. It's unbelievable. Not one of the kids could remember what happened. I was so baffled by that I had to find out myself what's going on up there and if this is really true, so I got some of my friends, who are also paranormal freaks like me who have to find out what's going on up there. So, I get all of us together, and we all talk about the stories we have heard from our parents and grandparents. We come up with a plan where to meet up in the morning, then we can check things out, look around, and see if we see anything strange and do a little investigating. As we drive through the first driveway, it's up a little hill with old maple trees hanging over all the old stones from back in the 1900s. This part of the cemetery is really spooky and dark. We then drive around the circle that brings us to the top of the new section, which puts us up on top of the hill. We can see all over the town and for a ways. We all get out. It's a beautiful summer's day; birds are chirping. It's actually really nice up there. Then we see the caretaker mowing the lawn down below. We go over and talk to him. He notices us and comes over.

"Hi, kids. How are you?" We all say good, and he recognizes us and asks how our parents are doing, and then asks us how can he help. We then tell him about the stories and rumors, and he pauses for a second, looks at all of us, and says, "Kids, they are all true."

We all look at each other and swallow hard.

He then said, "While mowing, I see things that are strange and hear stuff. Nothing has ever happened to me, but then again I don't come up here at night. I refuse to. It's a strange place at night." He then said, "You guys aren't thinking of doing that, are you? Are you? Come on, guys. This shit is dangerous. I'm not kidding."

We told him we are investigating today and MIGHT do that later, but we aren't sure.

He then said, "I'll say a prayer for you guys, because something will happen. It's not that it won't, it will. I guarantee it. He said, "This place at night isn't very nice. It's dark and dangerous. Please, guys, be careful. Go in groups. Stay together."

As he left, we all look at each other like, "Holy shit, this just got real."

As we walk back up to the car to get our things, it just feels weird, and the others in the group feel the same way, like we are being watched. As we walk around, looking at the trees and things in the woods, we notice like there are trails or deer paths. We didn't go toward them, but that's what they look like. We then take the drone and fly it overhead to see if we can see where they are going, plus what's over the tree line. As we are watching the drone, we are videoing the area also and seeing if we see anything that sticks out, just then what looks like a rock is thrown at the drone, and then another one. We go higher to see if we can find out who or what threw the stones, and nothing. We then bring the drone back, and it's all marked up with rock marks. We all look at each other and just are amazed at that. We then hear this loud noise coming through the trees and bushes. We are like, "What is that!" It's so loud and what sounded like a loud growl or a *grrrrrrrrrrr* just then it's silent. No birds, no squirrels, nothing. It's so quiet. I look at everyone else and say, "Let's get out of here. This is weird right now." So we all head to the car and get in and start to leave. When we are going around the back half of the cemetery, we all get a look at this dark like shape in the bush. We can't make out what it is, but we all see something. We get home and take the footage of the drone and start looking at it to see what's behind that thick bush, and as we are looking, we notice something on the video it's about where the rocks started to get thrown at it, we see what looks like a man figure, and the bad part is, it's tough to make out and see. But we know now we have to go and check this place out tonight. We all agree that we have to. Someone threw those rocks, and what we noticed in the bush when we were leaving, plus the feel of that place. It's creepy.

We all agree tonight we are heading back to investigate, but we need to pair up, two or three people in a group. Just in case there is someone there, we have extra people to help out. We also agree not to leave without someone with you. So, as we wait for the night to arrive, we get all the stuff ready, our cameras, our extra batteries, etc. So as night falls, we get all our stuff ready for the investigation. We pull in, and it looks really eerie. There is only one light lite way up on top of the hill where we parked the cars. We make a tent; that's where homebase will be. We get everyone all set and we get in our groups. I then say, "Okay, we know this place is nuts, and dangerous, so stay with your groups. If you see something, start yelling or whistle and we will come running. We all have two-way radios on us, so please stay together and keep your recorders rolling, okay? Be safe. Let's go."

So as we start and walk down to the old section in the front of the cemetery, we notice that it's super dark and very quiet down here. Just then we here this *bang*; it sounded like a tree limb had fallen, but then we hear the sound of someone running in the dry leaves. We shine our flashlights over in the spot, but nothing. That got our attention. Damn, this place is spooky at night. I grabbed my two-way and asked the group on the other side of the cemetery how it was going, and they were having a hell of a time. As we heard running, they saw this mass figure up on top of the hill in the moonlight, and we just started investigating.

As we started up the road, we were asking some questions about who the shadow man was. Is he real, and man, that wasn't what we should have asked. We see this mass/figure up in the road ahead of us. We shine the flashlights and see what looked like fog or a mist. All of us go like, "Did you see that?" and just like that, it's gone.

Just then one of the guys jumps back and yelled, "I WAS JUST TOUCHED!" He starts to run. We all run after him and tell him to get ahold of him selves and to calm down. He said, "It grabbed the back of my arm."

Holy shit, this is crazy. As this is going on, the group on the other side were dealing with the same stuff. They were following this dark mass. They would see it for a second, then it would go away, and then it shows up in another spot. As they were walking to where they saw the mass, it headed right for them, and they all dove to the ground, so as not to get hit with it, loud screams and banging sounds all over the place. They call us and say that they have had some really weird stuff happen. We tell them about the grab, and we all agree to meet at the car to go over some of the evidence.

When we get there, each group is telling the other what they experienced and how wild this place is and what's going to happen next? We hope nothing we don't want anyone hurt. Remember, this is still a dangerous place. If you see someone or something, shine that flashlight in their eyes and run like crazy.

We all decided that the back half needs to be checked now. "That's the place where all the noise was coming from, so, everyone, be careful, stay in your groups, and don't get lost."

As we split up, it feels really weird. It's dark and really quiet this time as we head toward the back end of the cemetery. We look over and notice the lights of the other group fading out as they head over to the other side. "Good luck, guys." This time it feels all wrong to be out here. As we clear the last row of headstones, we hear this growl so loud that all of us stop in our tracks and wait and look around. We then hear the shrubs moving right in front of us. Some of us move back, some of us are frozen in our tracks. We really can't see that great even with our flashlights; it's so dark. Just then I see what looks like an arm coming out of the bush, going to grab one of our guys. I yell, and he jumps out of the way just in time. Then we hear what sounds like running away from us, so we all look at each other and start going after it. The other group sees what looks like a shadow of a man, and they also go after what they think is a man figure. We go through rough, thick bushes and shrubs, then we come to a clearing, and we are stunned at what we see. It's a thin hut made out of the think bushes and trees. We then notice the other group way down to the left of us, and they look over and shrug their shoulders, and we yell to them, "Did you see anything?"

They say, "Nope, not sure what we saw." Just then, in between us, a huge, black cloud moved out of the bush and headed for the cemetery. Some of us stayed at the site, some took off after the mass. I was yelling to stay together, but everyone was so pumped that we lost both groups and the people down with me who stayed to look at the hunt stayed together and were taking pictures and trying to figure out what this was. Was it man-made or a trick by some people?

Just as we were ready to leave, we heard someone's name getting yelled at, and we headed back through that thick brush to find the rest of the team around two of our friends, and they both look like they are frozen. Definity something happened to them. They are out of it, and they just look forward and stared straight ahead, just like the graveyard guy told us. They don't talk and just stare, so we asked a couple of people to take them out of here and bring them home. We are now down to one group, and they are pretty scared, as I am.

"Let's get the recorders out and let's start recording and taking pictures of the whole thing."

As we walk around the cemetery, it has that feeling again like we are being watched, but I don't turn. I'm just recording. As I scan the cemetery, I hear things moving and sounds, but I don't move. I just record the whole lower half, then I run like hell to the top, fearing for my life. We then do the same thing to the middle and lower end. As we are walking back, I get that feeling like something or someone is close. The air changes, and just like that, I feel one of my draw strings on my hoodie go up like someone flicked it. I give out a yell, and everyone starts running toward the car.

"That's it," I said. "I'm done. That was unreal."

They all ask me what happened.

I told them I felt different. Just as I said that, one of my drawstrings lifted right straight up. "See if it's on the video." I was too nervous to look. I just wanted to get out of that place and go home.

As we are leaving, it feels like we lost. We had so many encounters with whatever is up there, and a couple people are sick or whatever they have or what was put on them. It's a feeling of unease. We get back to the house, and the two that were affected are doing better. As we all sit down and talk about what had happened and what experiences we all had, I then asked the two to try and remember what had happened to them.

They both look at each other and can't it's a blank. They both remember heading into the thick brush. "We opened it up, and now we are here. It's like it's erased from our mind."

I told them, "In the next weeks or however long it takes, if you could try and remember, that would be great." I then told the rest of them, "After they left, we went and recorded the whole area of the cemetery, and it's going to take a while to go through all of the videos and all of what you guys captured, so let's all meet here next week."

As I go over the footage, I'm blown away by what we didn't see as we were walking around. It's unbelievable. There is no doubt in my mind that there is someone or something up there, and it's not real. I call the gang, and we all meet up, and I have footage for everyone. everyone had one type of touch, saw something, or was affected by something.

We start off the very first time we are walking down on the front of the cemetery. Someone gets touched, but look what we see out of one of the guys' recorder as we all are running away. The recorder moves down to her legs as she is running away, and we all look at what looks like a man in a dark black suit just standing there. We are all alike, "No way. Holy shit, that's crazy!"

"Oh, it gets better. As the group is in the back, and they see that big mass coming at them, watch the first camera." As he goes down with the group, the camera picks up what looks like a man floating by. We all are like, "Oh shit! That's crazy!"

"You can see his head, upper body, and his hand trying to grab you guys. Unbelievable! The last two things are just before we all run into the bush, so listen really closely at this. You hear me say, 'Let's go,' and then this. We hear a voice that says, 'Come get me.'"

We are like, "Wait, play that again." So I did, and they all freak out. "That's creepy."

"Oh yes, he wanted us to follow him. Last one, and this is just the best. As I am scanning the area on the last day, I go back and forth, and then, just as I am ready to put the camera down, look over to the right."

The room becomes silent as they see a full-body apparition standing in the bush, just watching me!

"That's crazy!"

Then I go back with the camera, and it is gone. No one is there. I tell the group, "This is one place I will never come back to."

Both of the kids spoke up and are still affected. That one hour is lost to them. They don't know what happened, and they both have been having the same dreams. They are lost in the bush, and all they hear is a man telling them what to do like they are robots. They are still dealing with problems. They are going to seek some professional help. This place is exactly what the caregiver said it was going to be. Dark and Dangerous.

The End

Double Vision

One day, this young boy named Kyle was riding his bike around his neighborhood and came across this yard sale at the weirdest house on the block. It was a very old house, and apparently, the man staying there passed away. He was always walking around the block every day. He would walk, and he always looked angry, and rumor had it that he was a millionaire, and he had no family, and he walked all over the place, but people said he had two new cars in his driveway. It was weird to see him. He never said anything. Well, as the boy was looking at the stuff, it all looked super old and dusty.

He came across some older baseball cards in this nice wooden case. He asked the people who were taking care of selling the stuff how much for the baseball cards."

The person there said, "Twenty bucks for the entire case."

He said, "Can I save it over here, and I'll be right back. I have to go and get my money."

She said fine, and when he got back, the lady wasn't there, but he told the other person working what she saved for him, and they went to go and get it and came back with a bigger case. The kid didn't say a word, just grabbed it and headed home.

He went up to his room and started opening up the case and was so surprised there were some old clothes a lot of the baseball cards and other stuff deep down in the case. As he is looking through the rest of the stuff, he comes across a pair of these old glasses. They look like they are from the fifties, and as he cleans them up, he feels a vibration through the glasses, like he just turned them on. He places them on his face and *Bang!* Whatever he was thinking about, he was there, or at least he was seeing it. He immediately took them off. It was so weird, but then put them on again, and he started to understand how they worked. If he wanted to go to Germany, he thought about it put the glasses on, and he was there, it was the coolest thing. That night, he traveled everywhere. From one end of the world to another. It was amazing, until he became tired. He took the glasses off, and it was a little tough. It was like the earpieces were stuck, but he didn't think about anything else but to go to sleep.

He was super tired.

The next day, he was too busy, so he left them, and he would use them tonight, but all day he thought about them. It was like he was addicted. His mind was going in overtime, just to go and put them on. So that night, he was worried if something was happening to him, so he looked in the case to see if there was anything about the glasses, and all he found was pictures of his guy, and with every picture this guy was wearing the glasses. It was weird. The kid thought the same thing, so he dumped the entire case on the floor, and when he did, the bottom paper on the case fell out, and underneath was this letter. He read,

To whom it may concern,

You have a one pair of two glasses. Be very careful with them. If they break, that's it. You see, I designed them, and as you know, they are awesome. They work with your brain waves, imagining what your eyes see is reflected in the glasses. It took me years to develop and my family fortune, but man, they are awesome. Enjoy them, and remember to be super careful. If you're reading this, I am no longer present. Please take care of them, and if you know of someone who can try and duplicate them, you would be a rich individual.

Yours in science, Cedric Von Grober

Well, now I know how the glasses were made. The young man then had an idea: he would remember a place on the picture and see if he could find that man. It was a wacky thought, but it just might work, so he finds one of the older pictures and finds that it's in Tuscany, Italy, so he thinks really hard and puts the glasses on, and just like that he's walking around Italy. He laughs because it's so true how cool these things are, and just then, over in the distance he sees the man. As he runs towards him, the man goes around a corner and is gone. The kids takes the glasses off and is back in his room. *Damn, where did he go?* He grabs another picture and off he goes. This time. He was in Mobile, Alabama, but he just missed him, but the man turned before he left and looked at him with a grimace look on his face.

That night, the kid tried several places but was always behind the man in the pictures. So the next day, he goes to the library and looks up this Cedric Von Grober to see what or who this man was, and the kid was shocked. He looks just like the man in all the pictures. The kid then was confused but knew what he needed to do is find Von Grober, but how?

That night he took all the pictures out, and there were only a couple of them that he had not been to. As he lay on his bed, he had a brilliant idea. "Let me start all over and go back to the first place I went to or thought of." Just as he puts the glasses on, he tries to hide or blend in, but he doesn't know where he is. It's a place that he has never been before, but nothing is coming back to him.

Just as he is looking around, someone grabs his arm and says, "Don't look back. I have a gun pointed at you. Look forward and start walking.

He said, "What's going on here?"

The guy asked, "How did you get those glasses? who gave them to you?"

I told him the whole story, and he said, "Do you know Von Grober?"

I told him I don't, I just found them, then he told me when I take them off, destroy them. "I don't want to see you again, or you're gonna pay, kid. Just like that, he has me take them off, and just before I do, I look back, and it's the guy I have been looking for.

I see him and I then put the glasses back on and start running. He starts to chase after me, but I escape and try to find out where I am, when, just like that, I'm running near a train station somewhere in Germany. I think now that the guy wants to find Von Grober. This is getting dangerous. So I take them off, and I'm on my bed, trying to catch my breath and trying to figure out why he wants me to destroy the glasses. I then fall asleep on my bed and wake up to someone holding their hand over my mouth. It's the guy that was chasing me.

He shows me a gun and says, "Put the glasses on," and he holds onto me, and just like that we are in Germany again. He takes me by the arm, and we head over to this old hotel where he is staying. He sits me down and starts asking me again. He says, "Tell me the whole story. Where did you get the glasses and who gave them to you, and don't lie, kid, or you're done."

I go through the whole story again. I don't leave out anything, and he sits there and says, "So you never met Von Gorber?"

"No, I never did."

"See, kid, I'm stuck here. After a while, you can't take the glasses off. They get stuck to your face, and the only person that can help me is Von Grober. I'm sorry for scaring you, but I had to know what you knew. Be careful with those glasses, kid. They are very dangerous."

Kyle feels for the guy. "See," he said, "I applied for this cleaning job at Von Grober's house, and then Von Grober used me as his guinea pig, trying on all kind of glasses, and the last pair stuck to my face, and they sent me to Germany, and now I can't seem to get back to his house. These glasses won't take me there, and I can't think about it because they will just send me to wherever I'm thinking. It's so hard. I have to fight it off, and it's draining, but if not, I'll be everywhere. I must find Von Grober. He's my only help."

Kyle said, "I'll help you."

The guy said, "You will?"

"Yes. I feel for you man. I just want to take these things off. Where do we start?"

"Hmm, I guess let's go back to the closest place to Von Grober's."

"Okay, hold on." We are then transported to this old, run-down house.

I asked him if this looked like the house. He wasn't sure, so he started to go in, then stops.

He said, "We are close."

"How do you know?"

"Because look what the glasses are doing." They were moving on his face and kind of moving him in the right direction. We turned and started letting the glasses bring us to the right place, which was down about three blocks to this old, run-down house, and that's where we stopped. I looked at him, and he said, "We're here."

I was having a hard time processing this all, but I followed him inside, and it was like no one lived here, dirty, messy, and dusty. We go through all the rooms. No one. Then we see what looks like the basement door. We open it,, and there are lights on down below. We enter, and just as we get halfway down, we hear, "So you boys made it. I was wondering when you would."

We still couldn't see anything because of the stairs, but when we finally got down there, it was like a small workshop, and there stood Von Grober right in front of us, an older man, but one of those guys that looks really smart, with slacks on and a dress shirt with a lot of stuff in his right pocket, pens, paper, and small tools in it. He says, "Well, hello, Kyle. How are you?"

I said, "Good."

He then said, "You must have a lot of questions for me."

I moved my head up and down. Just then the guy whom I still have no clue what his name is runs at Von Grober and grabs his shirt and pushes him up against the wall. He says, "I want these glasses off. I hate this. I can't remember anything, and I want my life back."

"Easy, Brad, easy. It's just a little glitch. I will take them off you," and Brad then had settled down. Von Grober goes over to a small handheld machine and sits Brad down. He said, "This will help you take off the glasses." Von Grober then says, "This is the only issue I have with the glasses. I'm working on that."

Just as he does some adjustments, the glasses finally come of Brad's face. He has a marker of what looks like sunburn where the glasses were. He finally says, "Yes, I'm free."

Von Grober looks at him and says, "Okay, when I remove this from your head, you will be back at your place, and you will never remember what has happened to you. After I send Kyle back, I am going to destroy the glasses. The world's not ready for these just yet."

Brad looked at Von Grober, shook his hand, and he waved at me, and once Von Grober turned off the machine, Brad was gone. He then turned to me, "Kyle, do you have your glasses?"

I said yes.

He then said, "Put them on and let's get you home."

Kyle did as he was told, and Von Grober turned the machine on, and Kyle asked him, "What's going to happen to you?"

Von Grober then turned the machine on and took Kyle's glasses off. Von Grober then smiled at Kyle and said, "I'm just going to have to get two new people," as he hears Von Grober laugh, and just like that, Kyle is gone.

The End

Freaky

I guess you can say it all started when I came home from the space museum. See, I won these tickets and had a behind-the-scenes view of what's it like before people come to the museum. They just got this spaceship from the Space Center, and it just came back from space. I was so infatuated about it, and they didn't clean it up. It's just like they found it. I was rubbing my hand around the side of the ship, and all of a sudden I hit a piece of the ship where there was a sharp piece of metal sticking out, and it jammed right in my hand. I pulled it back, and it was bleeding a lot. I went to the bathroom to get a paper towel, and all of a sudden I remember hitting the floor. Then I woke up. It's like two to three hours later. What happened to me? Did I passed out? I was so confused, but I just told myself that was it and then went back into the museum. People were asking me where I went, and I told them to just walk around the place.

That night when I got home I parked my car, and it was really dark out, but for some apparent reason I could see just like it was during the day. I had the hardest time going to sleep that night, and when I did, I dreamed about being on that spaceship and feeling the ship coming down from space into the Earth's atmosphere. I woke up, and it was so weird. I felt like I wasn't myself. I was having an out-of-body experience. As I walked around at work, I could feel my skin crawl, at least that's what it felt like. I also could see what was going to happen before it happened. My friend's coffee mug was placed on the side of his desk, and someone walked by and accidently hit it, and there was coffee all over his desk. I then come out of it and walk by his desk and push his cup over, and just after that someone trips and heads right for his desk, and if the coffee cup was there, it would have been a disaster. They all look at me and say, "How did you know that was going to happen?"

I didn't even think about it; it just came out of my mouth. "Well, he did have it on the edge of the desk, duh!"

As I walk away I was like, "Did I say that?" Hmm, I couldn't believe that came out of my mouth. I went back and apologized to him.

He said, "Man, that was pretty harsh."

I told him, "Yeah that's my bad. I haven't been myself lately."

"What's up?" he said.

I told him, "Ever since I came back from the space museum I haven't felt right, but it's probably a virus or something. I'm going to take the afternoon off and go home and sleep. I don't feel good."

"Okay, buddy. Feel better."

I got home and went right to bed. I didn't even take my clothes off. That night I dreamt of being in outer space. It wasn't scary; it was amazing floating around and then finally coming down to Earth. I then wake up at ten o'clock at night. I slept the whole day. I have never done that in my life. I felt so much better, and after taking a shower, I was going to go for a walk, just to get out of the apartment.

As I am walking, I notice that it's pretty light out. I could see for a mile I felt, but in reality, it was ten at night and black, but not to me. I could see just like it was during the day. It was weird. Then some of my friends were going to meet up at our favorite bar and wanted me to meet them there, so I was excited about that. I walk in, and the place to me is pretty bright, and I notice my friends who don't even see me. I'm waving, but nothing. I'm like, "What, they can't see me?"

I ask the guy next to me as I make my way over to them. "Boy, this place is bright tonight, right?"

He said yeah as he laughs, he then said, "Are you being sarcastic?"

I then said yeah.

He said, "I've never seen it so dark in here."

He walks away and I'm like, "Something is wrong with me. Why does it seem so bright? I almost have to put sunglasses on." So I do, because it's so hard to see. I then make it to the table.

The gang then said, "How can you see? It's like, pitch black in here tonight."

I just lied and told them I was wearing them for looks. They all laughed, but I was like, "Man, what's going on with me?"

I then can hear a conversation between two girls on the other end of the bar talking about me. I then think that their wine classes would leak all over their dresses, and just like that it happened. I started to figure this thing out. When I think about something, I can make it happen, so I try it again. This hot chick walked by me, and I was thinking about lifting up her skirt, and it happened. She screamed and was trying to pull it down. I smile and laugh. I can't figure it out, but it's freaky. So, as I think of something, and it happens, it's bizarre, and yet fun all at the same time.

My friends then say, "Let's get out of here and go downtown."

I was like, "I think I'm going to go home."

"Okay," they say, "we will see you."

As I am going home, I think a lot about what happened and how I got these powers or whatever they are. I then try to remember when this all took place. Just then two guys jump out of an alley and have a knife and say, "Give us all your money and anything else you have or we're gonna cut you."

I was so scared. Just then I was thinking that the knife was in my hand, and just like that the knife was in my hand. I then looked at them, and they were like, "How did he do that? Let's get out of here," and they ran off.

I was like, "YES, take that, bitches!" I felt so invincible. Unbelievable, what a feeling. As I walked home, I was trying to figure out how this power came upon me and what I did, and nothing was coming to mind.

The next morning, I woke up, and my hand hurt really badly. I look at it, and then it hits me! I cut my hand on the spaceship. Could that have done it? The area is so sore I can't hardly touch it. I then call my buddy who works at the museum, and I tell him everything, and he says, "You better get over here so I can look at it."

As I am driving over to the museum, I get this realization that I am in the spaceship again, coming down from outer space. I almost wreck, but I come out of it. I get to the museum, and he has me go in the back where all the microscopes are and puts my hand under one, and then I hear him say, "Holy shit! Look at this."

I put my head in the microscope and see this organism moving around in and out of my skin. I then start putting things together. I told my friend, "How are we going to get this out of my body?"

He said, "You have to have something that they want to go to. Well, you know how you had those powers, lol." Just then he has an idea. "Let's go back to the ship and tell me where you got cut." He brought this handheld microscope with him. I walked around the ship and felt myself drawn to one spot, and I pointed it right here. He looks through the microscope and finds more of that stuff, and just like that, I feel a burn, and out of my hand comes the rest of that stuff. I feel so drained, but just like that, it goes right back into the ship. It's like, attached to it. I then go back to the office and check to make sure nothing else is in me. I then have another revelation. It's like they were thanking me. It must have been a family or something, and then just as it started, it was gone.

The End

Friends

"Get in the car," he said. "It will be fun," he said. "We will go to the south," he said. It's all bullshit. The car breaks down. We walk for miles, and now we have no clue where we are. Yeah, this isn't fun. My friends wanted to head to the southern states for spring break. I was apprehensive because whenever we get together, there is always something that goes wrong, and one of us always pays for it. As we walk down this dirt road, we notice we are deep in southern Georgia, I think. We walk to this old store and are going to get something to drink and find directions, to the closes city I hope. As we walk in, it reminds me of a really old show on TV.

It's like walking into *Mayberry*. I chuckle, because it's just awesome. We then see who we think is the owner, but it's not. It's just someone who works there, and boy, are they from the South. We can hardly understand him. So, we asked him what's the fastest way to the city. He laughed and said, "A whole day."

I was like, "Where are we?"

He said, You're in Thomasville, Georgia. You're closer to go to Florida, if you're looking for a city, and that's a drive also."

We were like, "How did we get here?"

Just then the guy said, "Way back when you were driving through the last village, you should have stayed straight, but you turned. A lot of people get confused with the signs, and then you end up here. But you better get moving. You don't want to be around late at night around here. It's dangerous."

We said, "What do you mean?"

He said, "The people around here don't like newcomers hanging around, so they take them, and rumor has it you never leave."

"What do you mean we never leave?" and he puts his thumb under his throat and does the slashing motion. We are like, "You have to be kidding."

He said, "Nope, I'm not."

We were like, "Hey, we need to get out of here."

The guy then asks us, "What's wrong with your car?"

We told him, "It over heated and then shut off."

He said, "I'm done here in an hour. I'll help you guys out, but you're gonna pay me."

Oh, we all agreed. That was no problem, just get us out of here.

So as we head over to our car. We notice the back of the bed of his truck has blood on it. He says it's from the deer he killed yesterday, and not to be alarmed. So, we get there, and he starts looking at it and said, "See, this happened to all the people down here. The Georgia dirt is pretty think, and it clogs up your radiator, and your car overheats, so now we need to tow you to the store to get the water hose and wash/unplug that dirt out of there."

So we get to the store, and it's getting late at night, and this watering the radiator isn't working, so we say, "What are we going to do?"

He finally said, "Okay, you can hide in back of the store, but don't go anywhere. I'm not responsible for you, get it?"

We all agree, and he lets us in. We stay there for about three hours. it's now 1:30, and now shit starts getting real. We hear noises coming from outside, so I crawl up to the door opening, and we hear this man, Dwayne, say, "Hey, outsiders, I know you're in there come on out, let's have a talk."

Just as I looked, I see the guy who helped us, and he looks like he has been beat up pretty bad.

As I crawl back, I notice the side door is open to a room in the back. I go in, and it's like a pantry. I see food, emergency aid stuff, then, in the corner, handguns and two shot guns. YES. I tell the boys we aren't going down without a fight. "Let's load up. Come on." So we get all we can, and I have two of them go up on the roof and cover me and two in the back with handguns and I had one, so it here goes.

I walk to the door and open it up. I step out, and the guy comes closer. I said, "Your good there as I show my hand gun."

He said, Your buddy here is going to need some help. Come get him."

I said, "Nah, I'm good here. What do you want?"

He said, "Well, son, you're trespassing on private property. You're gonna pay." So one of his fellows started walking toward me, and one of the guys up on the roof shot at his feet. He jumped back.

I then said, "The next shot is at your head. He's got you in the scope. All I have to do is give the word and you're dead."

He said, "So you boys want a fight?"

I said, "No, we don't. All you have to do is leave us alone. We will leave without any problems, and you guys can go on your way."

He said, "You know I can't do that."

I said, "Then you're in a war you're not gonna win."

He laughs. "Just because you boys know how to shoot a gun? Look around. You're on my land. You won this battle, but you won't win the war, son. Watch yourself, boy, and he leaves with his gang.

We go over and pick up the guy that helped us. He's beat up pretty good. He told us to take his truck and get outta here. "'Because he's coming back with more people and guns, and you're gonna be in trouble boys."

I told him, "We have enough guys to cover."

He laughs. "He's gonna blow this place up. Let's go get your stuff and follow me."

So we go back in the rear of the building, and he opens up a concrete door; it's the shelter for tornados. We all head in. As we walk down into this concrete room that seems to have an old mildew smell, we make it to the back where there's lights and lanterns are. We light a couple of them up, and he looks around. "Close that door, and make sure you lock it. Then the rest of you help me take this plywood of the wall."

We were like, "What's behind there?"

Just then the plywood falls, and it's another door. We were in awe. It took three of us to open the door, and it looked like a tunnel. We entered and he said, "Make sure you close it tight."

As we are walking down through the tunnel, I notice that it has fresh air, and we hear things like rumbling, and we are all wondering where we are. Just like that, we stop. He said, "Don't talk. Listen. Shhh."

Just then we hear that loudmouth Dwayne yelling. We walk some more, and at the end, there is another door made of wood. We push it open and go through. We all got through, and he said, "Stay low and follow me." So we all walked around the hill and crawled up the side of it. We are now on the other side of the road; that tunnel went right under the road. It's awesome that we are far enough away to see all the action. Just like the guy said, he started to burn the place down, and we need to keep moving. We don't want to be found.

We move down from that place and head toward this really old barn way away from the road, and the guy said, "This is Papa's property. He won't come on here; he don't like my papa, and my papa don't like him. You're safe here for a bit. I'll go and get some food and drink for you fellas."

When he returned, his grandfather was with him. We all said thanks for having us stay here, and he was so nice. He said, "That guy is an piece of work. Don't mess with him. He will hurt you."

I said, "How did you get in a mess with him?"

He was on my property, poaching. I told him to take his cronies and leave." Then he said, "This is my property. I pulled out my forty-five and pointed right at his head and said, 'I don't think so,' then he left. Then one night, on my way home with some hay, he blocked the road. Said I needed payment to cross his road. I called all my farmer friends. They all came down with guns and extra people. He was clearly outnumbered, and a couple of them had assault rifles pointed at him. One move and he's dead. He looked all around and said, 'You all are gonna pay.' One farmer told him to shut his mouth, he's sick of it. Oh, and he had one of the assault rifles pointed at his head. 'Tell me.' Boys, I'll end it here." He didn't say a word; all his other boys dropped their guns. "We told him, 'Watch yourself, son. You never know when the Lord might be calling you. He told his boys, 'Let's go.' They left, and that's the last I heard of him. But you boys need to get the hell out of here. If not, you're gonna get in trouble. He's a piece of work."

"Okay, Papa, had a plan getting us outta here and to get that guy, so we were going to fill the hay wagon all around us and leave us in the center, so it looks like an full load, and it would get us out, and we would set him up."

Just as we are all ready to get the plan into action, here comes Dwayne up the driveway. He told us to stay down. Papa walks over and waits until he gets up the drive.

"You know, Dwayne, you're on private property as Papa puts his hand on his 45. Oh, by the way, I don't appreciate you beating up my grandson."

"That wasn't me."

"Yeah, but your jerks take orders from you." As he goes to get out of the truck, we hear a shot ring out, and a ply of dirt goes flying right near his truck. "I think it's best for you to stay in your truck. You're not welcome here son."

"I hear you're holding them fellas from the city."

Papa says, "Nope, not me. You might want to check up town; that's what the boy told me. Now you can leave just as you came in."

As he leaves he's yelling things at Papa like, "You'll get it," yet Papa's, "You wait."

Papa walks over. "You can't trust that son of bitch. He's a mean and nasty bastard."

The next morning, we started to put our plan into action. Papa started off with us in the wagon and had a couple boys with us one in the front one in the rear. As we hit the road, so far so good, then the other boys were going to set up a trap for Dwayne.

So, the boys figured out where Dwayne was and headed over there to get him preoccupied, so we could make our escape. Everything was going good until one of the Dwayne's cronies came behind the last truck and pushed them right out of the way, and they went off the shoulder of the road. We notice this and start pushing the bales of hay out on the road. They dive and dart out of the way. Then I said, "Let's send five or six." So we throw those out, and one gets caught under their truck, and they can't steer it, and off the road they go and fly into this ditch. Damn, that looked like it hurt. Then Papa gives us the thumbs up. We just have to get to the other farm, which is about two or three miles away.

Just as we crest the top of the hill, there is Dwayne heading right for us. Papa steps on it and said to hold on. We heading right toward Dwayne. The hay trailer starts to shake and swing, and he's not stopping. Dwayne is getting closer. Papa pushes it right to the floor. We are just about ready to head-on, when, at the last minute, Dwayne veers off and heads into some trees wide open. He hits the trees. His truck goes flying in the air and tumbles upside-down two or three times and comes to rest out in a field. We never stop.

As we pull into Papa's friend's farm, we all are like high fiving each other and praising Papa. That was awesome

Papa then said, "We will go and see if he's okay. You guys meet Gus, my best friend. He will take you to your car, and boys, get out of here."

We all thank Papa for his help, and we invite him to come to the city, dinner will be on us.

He said, "Thanks, boys. Don't be a stranger next time. Just come and visit. Take care, fellas. I'll see you on down the road."

The End

Invasion

Walking into a forest by yourself is probably not a good idea, right? Well, you see, I need a hand. My car just broke down, and I have no idea where I am. That's all I remember telling the officer as they found me in the middle of the road, wet, and there is no water anywhere around me, and I have sucker marks all over my body. I can't remember a lot of what happened.

The officer then said, "Try to close your eyes and see if you can remember anything." All I remember is taking that shortcut through the woods to get to the other road. Wait, I do remember really bright lights overhead, and that's it. They take me to the hospital, and the doctor does a test on me to see what those sucker marks are on my body.

As they come back in, I'm concerned about what they are asking me, if I burned myself or if I had cupping done to me recently, and I am like, "Nope, I was on my way home. The car died. I cut through the woods, and now I am here. I hope someone can help me out, Doc. What's going on? Why can't I remember? You have to help me! What's going on?"

He then said, "I'll be right back." He then comes in the room with two guys from the US Air Force, and they close the door and start asking me a whole lot of question. After I tell them I can't remember much, one of them shows me pictures, and I look at other people with the same sucker markers I have, and then the men tell me, we are going to bring you to our lab and do some testing on you to see if we can find out what they are and help you."

I agreed, not knowing what I was getting into.

As we leave the hospital, the two gentleman tell me that I have to wear a mask, so I don't know where we are going. I agreed, but for some reason they didn't put it on very tight, and I could see a little bit, so I just pretended to not see until they put me in the back of the ambulance, and then I could see, but it was all backwards, but I sort of knew where we were going.... AREA 51! As we went through the gates and headed into the base, it was unreal that I have a chance to be here, but then they took me down and wheeled me into this bunker, and it was dark and very dim, but I still could see a little. As we rounded a corner, I see this female doctor.

She said, "Is this the patient?"

"Yes," they said.

"Okay, take him into the examining room." She was very attractive, and I could smell her perfume as she walked by.

The guy behind me said, Hey! Can you see?"

I said, "No, no, but I could smell, and she smelled wonderful," and I heard her chuckle as they moved me into the room and put me on the table and took off my blindfold. It's very bright, and they then put these eye caps on me. I just could see shapes. I asked them what these are for.

They said, "This is what you will wear when you are around here got it...."

I said, "Yes, I got it."

Just then I could smell her again, and I said, "Hello, Doc How are you?"

She said, "I'm fine. The question is, how are you?"

I told her, "My sucker markers hurt, and it feels like they move."

She said, "Move?"

I said, "I'm not sure if it's just me, but that's what I feel. Hey, Doc, what are they?"

She then tapped my arm and said, "We will help you. Don't worry." She then gave me a shot, and that's the last I remember.

I am then in my room, lying down. It was so weird. As I get up and try to find myself, I hear a voice that says, "Leave the eye caps on!"

I was like, "No problem. I was just rubbing my eyes."

The guys then said, "If I were you, don't."

I then asked him how many people have this.

He said, "Several. Now stop talking to me."

I was like, "Okay, no problem" and I went back to sleep.

I get up to some loud noise going on right across from me, and it's not good. I don't see the shape of the guy in front of my door, so I take off the eye caps, and I see this poor guy getting beat, and his sucker markers are worse than mine. I then start getting nervous. What the hell is going on here? What are these marks! Then I see my guy heading over to his spot. I quickly put my caps back on, and he said, "Hey, get ready. You're going to see the doc."

I was like, "Okay, no problem."

As I walk through the hallways, I start figuring out the layout of the block we were in. I get into the examining room, and I can smell her again. I say, "Hi, Doc."

She said, "Hello, how are you? How's your marks doing?" as she takes my shirt off.

I told her, "They are okay. After that shot you gave me they feel better."

Just then an alarm goes off. The guy yells to me, "You stay here until I get back."

I hear the door close. I turn my head to where I think her face is and I ask her, "What are these marks? Should I be nervous?"

She whispered in my ear, "YES!"

I was like, "I still feel them moving. Is there something inside me?"

She said, "Yes, we think it's little aliens, and they are studying you. When they are done with you, they will destroy you and then move on to the next person."

I was like, "How do we get them out?"

She said, "That's what we are working on."

Just then she said, "Be quiet. He's coming back."

I was like, "Okay, thank you. By the way, my name is Todd." she said, "Hi, Todd. I'm Dr. June."

He came back and told her to finish up. "We have another one for you, much worse."

"Okay."

"He's already," and as I am going back to my cell, I hear a bunch of people coming in, and I hear one of them say, "We see something coming out of his stomach." I get back to my cell and sleep for the night.

I'm awake, with screaming coming from the examination lab, and just then the guy wakes me up and says, "Let's go. You need to give blood."

I was like, "Okay." As I head to the examination room, my eye caps are half on because he's dragging me. I'm half asleep, and I see him for the first time, and he looks like a mean-ass bitch of a man. I look down quick, and he puts me in the chair. I see the doc for the first time. She's beautiful, and we make eye contact, and she smiles at me as she fixes my caps.

He said, "What's going on?"

She said, 'Just adjusting his caps. You can stand over there. Thank you."

As she takes my blood, he tells her, "I'll be back in a bit, keep him here." She agrees, and he leaves, and I ask her if I am going to die.

She said, "Not if I can help it, but we have to move fast. Take these tweezers and start working on that sucker mark on your stomach. Whatever's in you comes to the surface, and when it does, grab it and pull it out, and it should die once it hits air. Then start working on the other. He's coming back." So she finished up on me, and I head back to my cell, and this time he didn't stay. He walked across the hall to talk to one of the other officers, and I started working and massaging that mark on my stomach.

A week or so goes by as I am getting most of them out of my body, and the people around me are dying every day. I have to go and see her, so I get led down the long hallway. This time I could see many steps and notice bright lights, and we turn left, then a quick right, and I smell her. Mmmm, she smells so good. I sit in the chair, and the alarm goes off.

He tells her, "I will be right back."

"Okay," she says, and when he's out of sight, she asked me, "How many have you gotten out?"

I told her, "All of them."

She said, "Really? How?"

"I massage them and then they come to the surface."

She said under her voice, "Is it that simple?"

I then ask her, "How many people are left?"

"Not many," she says.

I lift my eye caps and look deep inside her eyes and I tell her, "Let's you and I and the rest of us make a break for it."

She smiles, "But you will never escape from here."

I asked her, "How long have I been here?" and she said, "Two long years."

"Wow, really? I'm so ready to go, aren't you?"

She smiles at me, and I move in for a kiss, and I tell her, "God, you smile wonderfully!"

She laughed and said, "He's coming back."

I told her to think about it.

As the guard gets into her room, she says, "He's ready to go."

He said, "Adjust your caps," as he kicks me in the ass.

I say, "Sorry, sir," and I go back to my cell, thinking of a plan. That night while it's pitch black, I take the tweezers and open up my caps so I can see better.

The next day, we head to the examination room, and I don't smell her. I sit down, and there's a man's voice. He says, "Where's your pain?"

"My stomach," I say, and as he's listening, I ask him in a whisper where the female doctor was.

"She's gone," he says. "Now quiet before you get us both in trouble."

I'm sad, and I walk back to my room, and they are doing bed cleanings, and I see my mattress go out and my tweezers are in the mattress. As I start walking to my cell, he grabs me. "Where are you going?" We go down the stairs. "They want to look at you."

I told him I had enough poking and prying. He kicks me again and I say, "I would love to see you do that after I'm healthy, you jackass," and that's all I remember. I wake up to that beautiful smell she's back, but I'm not in the examining room. I go in and out of consciousness, and I hear someone say, "You better control yourself do you hear me?" and the soldier said, "Yes, sir."

"Now switch with someone else."

I raise my hand and give him the middle finger, and he's pissed as he leaves. The doc comes over, and I hold her hand. "I can't see. Doc, what's going on?"

"Well, you got a butt end of a rifle in your forehead and face. It's bad."

"That guy is an asshole, but I knew I could get him pissed, but not like this." I try to laugh, but she gives me a shot, and I am out. She comes to check on me every day. My room now is in the corner of the examination room. It took me two weeks to heal up, so I was able to see her the last day. Before I go back to my room, the doc comes over and checks me out for the last time and hands me a note.

"Read it later."

"Okay," I say, and I head back to my old room with a different guard, a much nicer guy.

I read the letter that says, "I'm in for the escape problem. It's just you and I. The other ten people are too weak and won't make it out."

I told myself, "It's time. Let's do this." So I start checking the new guy's schedule. I notice he sleeps a lot; around the time I go out, he's out, so if I can get him into a deep sleep.

So that week I went to the doc, told her the plan, and we are a go. She gave me something to put in his water, and he usually leaves it right next to the cell, and that's what I did. There was a commotion down the end of the hall, and this was my chance. Just as I was about to reach over the bars of the cell, I get slammed by the guard's billy club, the old guard that is.

"You think you're a smart ass, eh? When you get out of here, I'm gonna kick your ass!"

The other guard came over and asked him to leave, and he started to argue with him, and while that was going on, I slipped two tablets into the new guard's water bottle. The plan starts. Just as he sits in his chair, he's done. I push him. Nothing. I reach over and get his keys, open the cell very carefully, and I switch into his uniform, and I put him in my bed. I then head to the examining room, and I see the doc. Just as I was going to walk in, she gives me the eyes. I then head to the bathroom, which is right across from the room. Just then I hear two people leave, and then I go in. She grabs her purse, and we head out to her car.

She told me to leave the hat and face shield on until we are through the gate. She looks at me and gives me the sexiest kiss I ever had. "Let's go."

As we are heading out through the first gate, then the second one, I look into the mirror to see that terrible place go out of sight. "As far as they know, you escaped. I must go back. That's my life."

I get out of the car, and she goes one way, and I go the other, and that's the last I saw of that lady. She saved my life. If not, I wouldn't have made it. Two years have gone by since the escape, and I work for a construction company, and I get paid under the table, and I stay off the grid because I know that once I pop up, I'll be done. I still have those marks to remind me what happened. I don't tell people because they wouldn't believe me even if I did.

The End

Johnny Boy

I guess you could say that it was a fantastic childhood, and what a great memory it was to grown up to. You see, Johnny Boy was more than just a friend, he was like family to me, and when he left, it was like I lost a brother. I guess I should start from the top and tell you who he was. You see, when I was a little boy, about ten, my parents moved us to a new house. It was much older house, and each kid had their own room; my brother Jim and sister Pam had rooms right next to mine. The first night in my room was a little different. See, my closet didn't have a door, and I swore after I was in and out of sleep, I saw someone who looked like a young kid, but I was so tired I wasn't sure.

The next morning, I get up and all my matchbox cars are all over the floor of my room. I was like, "My brother was in my room. Come on, Jim." But I go to his room, and he's not even up yet. I scratched my head, and then I just let it go.

That day we played outside all day, and at one time I looked up at my window, and I saw this little boy's face. I then head into the house and up the stairs and find no one. I was so sure I would have found someone, but nope, nothing.

That night, as I am drifting off to sleep, I try my hardest to stay awake, but it doesn't happen, and just before I go to sleep, I see what looks like a kid again coming out of my closet, and that's it. I fall asleep and wake up with all my toy cars all over the floor again. I was like, "This is nuts. Who's doing this?" I go and peek into my closet, and just as I get around the corner, a stuffed bear hits me right in the face. I scream and run out of my room and run right into my brother's. Ugh. I lie on the floor, and he's like, "Why are you running?"

I told him about the whole story, and he said, "I don't believe you." So that night I told him to come over and you'll see.

So that night, we both watched the closet entrance to see if this kid is going to come out. As we start to go under, I don't notice him, but just then my brother jumped up and yelled. I saw him. I get up, and we both go toward the closet, both of us really scared, not knowing what to except, and we peek in together, we see way back in the corner is a silhouette of a little boy. He doesn't say anything, just looks over at us, and my brother then says, "Hi, I'm Jim, and this is Gene," and just then the kid says, "Hi, I'm Johnny Boy."

We were like, "Where did you come from?"

"I've been in this house for years. I died here a long, long time ago, and I can't seem to leave."

"Well then,' I said, "let's play."

He then said, "I just can't be seen by your parents."

I looked at my brother and said, "That's okay. We will have so much fun, Johnny Boy," and we did. We played inside with him and did a lot of stuff outside. problem is, he can't go outside, so he was limited, but we still had a lot of fun. When school started, he stayed in the closet, but my brother played with him a lot, being that he was much younger than me.

He said they played pirate ship, and sometimes Mom would come upstairs and ask Jim why he was laughing so much, and one time Jim said, "Johnny Boy, Mum. He makes me laugh," but Mum couldn't see Johnny Boy, so that made Jim laugh because Johnny Boy would mimic Mum sometimes.

That winter we had so much fun with Johnny Boy, playing in, movies and pretend TV shows. It was awesome. He became like a brother. It was so much fun with him.

Then one day Mum came to us and said that we we're moving again. See, my daddy was in the military, and we moved a lot, and we were both so sad. Johnny Boy came out that night, and we told him what was going on and he was okay with it.

He told us, "I'll always be with you guys. Just imagine me." He then said, "No crying. We are flying across the world tonight in a hot air balloon."

That night it was so fun with him.

The next day we were moving and we never did see Johnny Boy because of all the moving going on, people in and out of our room.

We all got in the car and headed out to our next place. Who knows where that will be. As I wake up, I see a lot of countryside, and I'm so happy it wasn't a city, and the house was huge, and Jimmy and I ran right into the house to pick our rooms, but Mum said Pam had the first choice because she's a girl. Rats. So Jim and I were on the third floor. Fine with me. Our rooms were together, but a very small closet, and for the first week we kept the door open, and nothing.

Jim then turned to me and said, "I miss Johnny Boy."

"So do I, pal."

A couple more days go by when we hear this noise upstairs. Jim looks at me and I at Jim, and we both run up, and there is Johnny Boy playing with our toys. We were so excited he was back, and boy, what a time we had playing with him. We made forts, we played Cowboys and Indians. It was amazing. What a great year that was. He stayed with us for years, playing, laughing, and joking around, but the older we got, the less time it seemed we had. I was playing summer baseball, and Jim basketball, so we were so busy. When we got home, Johnny Boy was ready to play. We were just too tired.

The older we got the worse it was. We hardly ever played with him, and now it was like we were too old for him.

Then one night, he came out. He looked sad, and I asked him what's wrong. He said he was bored.

I then said, "Go wake up Jim. We're gonna play with the GI Joe guys."

He was so elated that he ran through the wall and right into Jim's bed, but then I heard Jim say, "Go away, Johnny. I'm too old for you. I need my sleep. I have a big game tomorrow."

That was the last time I saw Johnny Boy. He must have moved on. I told my brother, and he felt like crap, but he was just tired and didn't want to play. That summer we were so busy we never really thought about it. Then once fall and the holidays rolled around, I thought about him a lot.

As life moved us along and we now are older, one afternoon, my aunt came to visit with her two kids, a boy and a girl, Toby and Teya, my cousins, and my aunt kept asking us if we had an invisible person that we played with when we were young. Jim and I looked at each other, and we then went over to the kids and asked them a question about their invisible friend. They said that he's funny and loves to play and we do all kind of things.

I then said to Teya, "What's his name?"

She whispered in my ear and said, "Johnny Boy."

I had a huge smile came across on my face.

Jim was just like, "How's that happen?" but I was happy that the kids were having fun with him.

I told Teya to say hi to Johnny Boy for us. She said she would, and we left her to keep playing.

That night I sat in bed and thought of all the wonderful things we did with him, all the adventures and games we played. I looked at the closet and said, "Thank you, Johnny Boy, for a fantastic childhood."

The End

Mystery At The Fair

I woke up on one summer day so excited to head to the fair, not knowing what the day was going to bring, seeing it was a huge thing when you're eleven and you get to go all by yourself with just your friends. It was hot, but not a scorcher, so we pulled in and headed down the road to get to the fair, listening to Andy's mom yell, slow down, boys. Wait for me." So I guess I forgot to tell you. Hi, I'm Geno, and this is my adventure, the day we went to the Franklin County Fair. So, my friends Stephen, Andy, and Donny were brought to the fair by poor Andy's mom, Barb. She was a saint putting up with us. After we got our tickets, we left Andy's mom and started out on our own. The last thing I hear is, "Make sure you have your phones, boys." We all felt for them and gave Andy's mom a thumbs up we're good. As we leave Andy's mom in the dust, there is so much to look at. See, this is the biggest fair in our area, and it's a blast to see all the wild rides and things to do. We all saved up doing odd jobs to blow all our money at this place; it's awesome.

The first thing we head for is the wild and crazy human people: half man, half bull; the boy with two heads; the man with a snake for an arm. It's amazing but we know that it's all fake, at least some of us do, Haha. I still think Stephen believes in Santa Claus, lol. As we head over to THE CLAW, it's the craziest ride here, but man, you get big bonus points for riding it at our age, but the only one was Donny last year, and rumor has it he puked for two whole days after riding it. We all agree we are going on it. It's awesome. It has two poles with this huge beam that comes down in the middle of the poles. At the end of the beam is this basketlike device that you sit in; it starts to spin and starts to move back and forth until you almost go all over while you are spinning. Ugh just thinking about it makes my stomach sour. We all get in, pull the hold downs, and lock them into place, and it starts, and there is no looking back. We all scream, and when it's done, all four of us puke when we get done, hahaha. We are so pumped that we rode THE CLAW. Hell yeah we did it.

After we collect ourselves, we then start looking around to see what's next. I notice what looks like two guys talking, and one guy gives this other guy a package, which he puts in his pocket. At first, I didn't say anything to the guys because I was the only one that saw it, but it seemed to follow us all over the fairgrounds. Pretty much every time we went for a ride, there was an exchange. Not sure what was going on, but it started to worry me. After riding half the rides, we sat down to eat, and man, I was hungry, but once food touched my mouth, I almost puked. I couldn't do it. As I look over at Andy, he gets up really quick and heads for the trash can, hahaha. I guess I'm not only the one with a queasy stomach, but Stephen, it didn't stop him. He was tearing up the food. He could eat after anything, and poor Donny, he just looked green. We were all in trouble.

I told the boys, "I think we need to play some games now to settle our stomachs." They all agreed, and as we headed over for the games, I saw this one guy hand over something to the guy behind the food stand, and he caught me looking at him. I just then hurried up to meet up with the rest of the group, and the guy put two fingers to his eyes and then pointed at me, like he knew I saw him. I was scared and told my friends what I have been seeing, and they were like, "How come you haven't told us before?"

I was like, "At first it was nothing, then it kind of turned into something, I guess."

Stephen yells, "You guess? Now we got these guys on us."

I said no not you, just me." UGH! My stomach got sore again about what to do. We finally all agreed. After a while, no one was coming after us, so we did nothing and put it behind us, and we went back having fun.

It wasn't until around two-ish in the afternoon when things started to go south. See, we went on one of the rides that the guy who gave me the two fingers to his face was running. It was called The Mystic! It was awesome; it was a round, caged-in ride, and you sat in the middle of it, and you could spin it if you wanted to, and man, we had that thing spinning. We must of went around a dozen times, and we all get sick again, and it finally stops, and we get out. I'm so sick/dizzy I can't hardly see straight. All I remember is someone grabs me and we head behind the ride. He gets in my face and says, "What are you doing?" staring at me. "What did you see?"

I told him, "Nothing. I can't even see you now," as I throw up all over his feet and some of his pants.

He says, "Jesus, kid, watch out," and just like that, as I am puking, I hear another man say, "Leave him alone before he tells someone."

As I walk from out back of the ride, I find the guys calling my name and wondering where I was. I walked away and told the guys what happened. They said, Who were the guys?"

I told them, "I couldn't see his face. I was so dizzy." They all laughed at me because I puked all over him, and just like that we started to go over to other rides.

It's getting late in the afternoon, and we all go in the mirror maze, which is unreal because once you leave your partner, you're done. You will be in there for a while, and we all entered in different places, and we could see each other, but we couldn't touch one another. There was always a mirror in front of us, lol. It was so fun, until it was just Stephen and myself. Not sure what happened to the rest of the guys. I looked at Stephen and said, "Let's get out of here."

He said, "Geno, I'm nervous."

I told him, "Try to find a way out." Just then I hear him scream. I yell his name, and nothing. Just then I see this man. I don't know who he is, but he knew me from somewhere.

He says, "Geno."

I said, "Who are you?"

"It's not important. What's important is that what you have been seeing is nothing, just a couple guys passing notes to each other on how to run the rides, okay?"

I was like, "It looks suspicious."

He said, "Well, we don't want all the people at the fair to know what's going on with the rides or certain games."

I said, "Okay," but I was lying, and I said, "Okay, I'm going to go now."

He said, "Your friends are outside. If you need anything at all, you come and find me. My office is the trailer in front of the fair entrance."

I said, "Okay, and thank you." As I start to leave, I know something isn't right, but I just played dumb. As I get out of the Mirror Maze, I see all the guys standing there, and there are guys all behind them.

I was like, "Hey, guys. Everything okay?"

Just as I said that, two sheriffs were walking by. They say, Everything okay here, boys," and we all shake our heads, as the guys standing there take off in every direction.

One of the sheriffs asks, "Mr. Drinkgo, is everything okay with these guys?"

"Oh yes," he said, looking right at me. "I just had some of my guys go in and get these guys out of the maze. We heard screaming, so I got nervous."

"Okay, boys, you guys are okay?"

We all said thank you and we took off to go somewhere else. I started thinking about what Mr. Drinkgo told me, so, as we were walking, I told the guys what he said to me in the maze. They were like, "Holy shit, there must be more like, something else is going on here."

I was like, "I had enough of this place."

Stephen shook his head in agreement, but I was like, "I have to find out what's going on here. Mr. Drinkgo is hiding something; those guys aren't just passing letters to run the rides. Come on, guys. Something else is going on and we need to split up and find out what it is."

Andy and myself left to check on the rides that we already went on, and Stephen and Donny, even though they didn't want to, went back to the rides we just finished riding. I told the boys to look for clues, things in the trash etc. "They are looking for four of us, not two. We will meet in the middle of the fair at eight o'clock at the taco stand. Get it? Call us if you have something, and remember to stay with each other."

As we head away, Andy said, "What do you think we are going to find?"

"I don't know, but it's not notes they are passing, that's all I know."

So, as we head to the other side of the park, we walk, and we take it all in. It's just awesome music playing, carnies yelling at you to try your luck at the games you never win, and the lights. It's unbelievable at night. Oh, and the smell of fair food. Man, that gets me all the time.

As Andy and I head over, I tell him, "Keep your eye out for the carnies that run the rides."

Just as we walk past the Ferris wheel, Andy tugs on my shirt. He said, "I see one, but look at him, he's behind the gate to the ride, and it's like he's drunk." He was weaving back and forth over and just then he falls, but picks himself up. We both notice something falling from his pants.

We wait until he leaves, and we go over it a piece of paper. I tell Andy, "Let's go on the Ferris wheel and we can look at it up and take our time." So we get on the ride and it goes to the top, and as we open it up, it's directions and information about the package this guy was supposed to get. We then call the other guys and tell them to meet us near the taco stand again in like fifteen minutes, we have a HUGE clue.

We then asked them if they had seen anything, and they said, "We will tell you when we see you guys."

"Okay, sounds good." So Andy and I wait to get off the ride and head over. We get there and sit on the picnic table and we go over what we both have. Stephen and Donny overheard one of the carnies that they almost have all the packages. Not sure what that's means, then Andy told the boys, "We found this piece of paper, and it has these directions on it and where to go."

I was like, "This is awesome."

Donny said, "Let's go and get the package ourselves."

I looked at the rest of the boys and said, "Yeah, let's do it."

So the directions said, "Go towards the bumper cars and behind the gate there will be a little door. Open it up, and your package is there."

So we asked for volunteers no one wanted to, so we came up with rock, paper, scissor to win. First Andy and Donny went. Andy won, so then I went with Stephen, and I won. It was then up to Donny and Stephen, and poor Stephen lost. He was like, "No, no, no, no! I'm not doing it! NOPE!"

We all said, "Hey, you lose. Just wander over. If no one sees you, grab it and just walk over to us."

"Come on, let's go, Stephen."

He looks at us. "You guys better not leave me." We all agreed not to. As he walks over, there is no one around; he goes around the gate and then opens up the little one and grabs the bag. He looks at us. We motion him to come over there. Nobody's around. "Why" That was easy. We then opened the bag, and what we saw was a bag of money.

We were like, "WOW, there's millions in there," not knowing what millions looks like, of course. We knew then we had to do something, but what?

"We have to hide it," said Donny.

"You're right," I said, but then Stephen said, "I have a place." So we took the bag, which was like a backpack.

We follow Stephen to the Haunted House ride. We then go in. Stephen shows us a trunk where a zombie pops out, and just like that Stephen throws the bag inside the trunk. We leave the ride, and we all agree we need to come back and get it tomorrow. So, as we call Andy's mom to come and get us, we get this feeling that we messed up and we should have taken it back with us. So, as we get home, I text the other guys and ask them what are we going to do when we get the money. We all agreed that we would bring it to the Sheriffs, and then they would arrest the guys and we would be heroes. I guess it's what I thought of as I drifted off to sleep, but it didn't happen like that.

As we get to the fairgrounds, it's like ten o'clock, and there are a lot of people here already, so we buy our bracelets, so we can ride the rides for free, and we then split up and go on a couple, and then we would all meet up at the Haunted House, and it sounded like a great plan until Stephen and Andy went in the Haunted House and came out with nothing. They acted pretty cool and went right on the Ferris wheel that was right next to the Haunted House, and as they were up in it they called us, and we were playing a game when I heard both of them yell, "The bag is gone."

I was like, "What?"

They said again, "The bag is gone." We both looked at each other.

"Let's all meet up at the taco stand in ten," We all agreed, and Donny and myself were just at, and aw, we were like, "What do we do now?" Then Andy and Stephen get there, we all get something to eat; we just can't believe it.

"What do we do now, we look at Stephen and ask him, "You sure it's not in there?"

He says, "Yes, I checked."

So we said, "We are going to double check." So Donny and I head over, and as we are going into the ride, people get off the ride and scare other kids;

that's what you did. As I see Donny go over, he waits till the zombie goes up. He reaches inside, and way in the corner was the bag. He pulls it out and then runs over to the ride and jumps back in, just as an attendant comes in and starts yelling at the other kids to stay on the ride. He leaves, and Donny puts the bag in his bag, and we leave the ride, laughing and yelling, and we also head on the Ferris wheel, which is right next door, to see what's in the bag. As we get out of sight, we open the bag, and we see money. We are like, "YES!!"

Donny smiles at me and reaches into the bag and grabs a handful of it, and as he pulls it out of the bag... we both look at each other and say, "WHAT!" It's Monopoly money! We have been stiffed. I was so pissed. I couldn't believe it. We called the other boys, and they couldn't believe it, either. How did it happen? We just didn't know, but we knew somehow they knew, and they did the switcheroo on us, and who would believe us anyway, and if we said something to someone who would believe us, we knew what we found, and it wasn't Monopoly money.

We walked around the fairgrounds that afternoon, distraught and rejected. As we leave the fairgrounds, I see Mr. Drinkgo look at us and say, "Thanks for coming, boys," with a huge smile on his face. As we leave, I look back, and he puts two fingers to his eyes, then points to me. That day we all had so much fun. We knew that it was an adventure, and there's always next year, and we all can't wait to go back to the fair.

The End

Never Lost

Just after I turned nine, my grandpa gave me an older-looking pocketknife, I think it was an old Boy Scout knife. It had a picture of a bear on the front, with a deep blue covering the rest of the surface. The coolest aspect of it was that it had three different blades that you could pull out from the center. It never left my side growing up; I even brought it with me to church, making sure Meme never found out.

One day, while I was riding my bike to the barn, that beautiful blue knife somehow came out of my jeans and went flying out. As I got to the barn and started my chores, I was so distracted I didn't notice it went missing until I needed to cut the bailer twine and couldn't find my knife.

"Darn, where is it?" I whispered to myself as I continued to fish through my jeans anxiously. Each time, my hand returned empty, and there were no spaces left for it to be hiding. I was devastated. I lost the one thing my Pepe gave me.

I ran out of the barn and down to where the road was. I walked up and down the road, looking for my knife until it was dark outside. I went back into the barn and felt the dead weight become heavier as I laid eyes on my Pepe.

"What's wrong, son?" my pops asked.

I shook my head, but I knew they could tell something was wrong. I quickly finished up my chores and headed back home, feeling guilty and lonely without my knife.

Days and weeks went by, and nothing popped up. I looked and looked and could not find that knife. I almost gave up hope of ever finding it, when, one day, while I was mowing the lawn, I noticed a shiny thing in the grass that I mowed over. I got off the mower and reached down deep in the grass and pulled up what at first looked like a coin. After turning it over in my hands a few times, I was surprised to see my blue knife I lost a month ago staring back at me.

"WHOOPIE!" As I laughed and cheered, I couldn't believe my eyes. I was overjoyed. I then ran to the shed and started to clean it up. After I got it back to its original look and feel, I kept it back in my right pocket where it belongs.

As the years went by, I still used my knife all the time at the barn, and also when I was working on cars and cleaning up the grounds. One day, I was mowing the lawn at the barn in shorts because it was so hot out. Somehow, once again, the knife fell out of my pocket, and just my luck, I didn't notice it until the next day. Just as I was reaching into my pocket for the knife to cut some of the strings I had attached on the truck, I couldn't find my knife I had the eerie familiar anxiety settle in.

"What's going on? Where is it?" I angrily muttered to myself, once again searching for something that wasn't there. It had been so long that I had that knife, and now it was gone once again.

I was so upset with myself, but I needed a knife to cut the strings on the truck, so I took a short ride to the hardware store, McGregor's. I found a new knife, small like my blue one, just to get me by. I had that second knife for about two months until I broke it trying to pry on something. By that point, I was starting to give up trying to find my blue knife because I had no idea where it could possibly be. I was out two knives, and the summer was slowly melting away, with hopes of ever finding my blue knife again.

I was mowing for the last time before the weather turned and decided I'd clean the mower up before locking it in the shed for the winter. I drive it over to the water hose and start cleaning it up. As I lifted the edge to get under the mower, a massive chunk of dirt and grass fell to the ground. I shook my head and drove the mower back into the shed and locked it up for the season. I walked back over to the water hose and wrapped it back up, but before I went back in the garage, I looked back at the chunk of dirt and grass that fell on the ground from under the hood of the mower. I shrugged my shoulders and grabbed the chunk to throw into the woods but stopped in my tracks when I felt something cold and smooth rub against my finger in the dirt. I let go of the chunk instantly and looked down at it, wondering what I had just felt. I finally got up the courage to inspect it a little more, and I'll forever will be grateful for doing so because as I moved the dirt and grass around, my eyes landed on my old blue knife I had lost two years ago.

"What!" I'm shocked, but start to inspect my knife. A bit rusty, dirty but overall, in great shape. I was so happy; it seems as if I could never lose this knife for good. It always comes back to me eventually.

As time passed, I kept an eye on that knife and made sure I didn't lose it again but, guess what happened. I was at the barn, and I needed to cut some string. Just as I reached into my right pocket, the knife was gone. I tried to retrace my steps that day, searching all over the barn for my knife, but I couldn't find it. I was devastated and couldn't believe I lost it for a third time.

"Pops, I lost the knife Pepe gave me again," I told my dad, knowing what happened would be safe with him.

"Don't you let Pepe know, he will be upset. You know he's up there in age." He shook his head and put his hand on my shoulder. All day we spent time looking for that knife, but we couldn't find it at all.

Time moved on, and eventually, I forgot about that knife. Life went by, and my Pepe passed away. I felt terrible for not having the knife when he was alive toward the end of this life. I end up going back to the farm to work, and on my way to the bulk tank one day, I'm thinking about life. My head is clouded with these thoughts, and as I reach into my pocket for the knife to cut the top of the grain bags, I remember it is not there. I feel an overwhelming sadness as it makes me think of my Pepe and the life he lived. I go to reach on top of the grain bend for a knife, and my hand comes in contact with something so familiar. I grasp it in my hand and bring it to my eyes and couldn't believe what I was holding. My knife had been sitting back there for who knows how long, but what a crazy coincidence it was to find it as I was thinking about it for the longest time..

To this day, I still can't understand why or when I left my knife in that spot, but I was so thankful to have found it once again. That night I lay in bed and prayed to the Lord that my Pepe up in heaven would know I found my knife that he gave me. I cherish that knife more than ever now, as it is his lasting memory I carry along with me in this world. His memories are what I see when I hold that knife, and I hope one day I will be able to pass it on to my grandkids to make their own memories of the time they have with me.

The End

Panic At Lincoln High

One day at our High School in Lincoln, Nebraska, it was science week, and man, it was going to be amazing because we were going against the other grades, and prizes were going to be giving out for the best chemical compound that each class could whip up, and of course, you had to use only chemicals that we had in science class. So, all the other classes went before us, the Freshman, Sophomores, Juniors and then, yes, us Seniors.

It was the seniors' time to shine, so we went in and started to look for what we were going to use. There were a lot of chemicals that other classes used, but we wanted to be different, and way back in the shelf, there were two bottles of this power chemical that had no name, so some of us were like, not sure what it was, but we wanted to use it.

Some of us said, "Hey, we should ask the teacher if we can," but we didn't, and we poured the whole two bottles in with the other chemicals and started to stir it up. As we notice, it turned a dark blue from the powder, and it starts to grow. We all are yelling and clapping. We thought that we were going to win this, but boy, were we surprised. It started to grow quite rapidly, and we all were like, "What's happening with this?" It's really growing way too fast, and just like that, it grabbed one of the baseball players who was just standing there, and it surrounded him, and it engulfed him. We tried to grab him, but it was too strong, and then it started to fill the room.

We all yelled. The closest people to the door were the ones that got out first, but some of the others weren't so lucky as it overcame them, and it looks like it suffocates you.

"AHHHHHH, I can't believe this! "It's unreal. Why does this stuff happen?"

As we come running out of the room, the foam is filling up the room, and it starts coming out, and we are all yelling, "Run!"

Some of the teachers were going over to see if they could close the doors. I yelled to them, 'It's going to consume you, just run."

They stopped in their tracks and took our advice, and we all headed to the cafeteria and waited for the science teacher, Mr. Roberson, comes over and says, "What did you guys do?

We told him.

He then puts both hands to his head and says, "That was the accelerant growth power that we used on the regrowing dead plants." It must of had a chemical reaction to the other chemicals. He said, "Okay ,what did you mix it with?" and we all tried to figure it out, but some of us weren't paying attention when the other kids put the stuff in. He looked at us. "This stuff is just going to keep growing. It's designed to eat things, that's how it survives. It must consume things."

I then said, "If we can get into the gym, there's nothing there for it to eat."

Mr. Roberson said, "That's not a bad idea Jonah, but how to get it there?"

Just then the front door of the cafeteria is knocked down, and here comes the foam, and man, it looks bigger than before. We all head out the other end and of the cafeteria and make our way to the hallway wing that leads us to the music room. As we take a break there, Mr. Roberson grabs a sheet of paper and starts working on some formulas for a counter. He then slams his hand down. "I can't think right now."

Just then the door of the music room slams open, and there is the foam coming in and heading right for us.

Mr. Roberson then yells, "Quick, out the back door!" and he closes it behind us and that puts us in the swimming pool area. We now know we have to get out of here. The girls' locker room or the boys', so we sit and rest, and it doesn't take the foam long, here it comes. It heads right for the pool, but there is no water in it, so we think for a second, "We have it," but it fills up that pool really quickly, and we head out of there and head for the locker rooms.

As we make our way through the locker rooms, we somehow lose the girls. They must have went through the girls' side. As we get to the end and go through the open door, Mr. Roberson pushes it back and just like that. He then yells, "Hurry up and follow me."

Just as we go through the other door of the locker room, we come just in front of the foam, which now doesn't seem to be moving too fast, which it's weird. Just the girls come out, and Mr. Roberson yells, "The side door! they slam the door, and then we see them come out the other side. We are all back together.

I ask Mr. Roberson, "Why is it slowing down now?"

He looks at all of us and said, "I think we can shrink this thing. Let's go to the—" and just like that, we were trapped, because around the corner there's more foam. We all start to run for the exit, which is down the hall. The doors are locked. we all scream, then we see Mr. Roberson take a chair and smash the door glass, and we get out just in time. We all stand there, and it doesn't come after us, like it knows something. We were all baffled about this. Just then, we see Mr. Roberson running alongside of the building; he yells to us to come on. We follow him around to the front side of the school, where we are standing right in front of the science class.

It looks abandoned except for the people that got sucked up in the foam. Mr. Roberson said, "We need to get inside and get some chemicals I need.: So we go back get the chair, and he slams the glass to get into the room. It's dark, hard to see, and it has a weird smell coming from the inside. Mr. Roberson said, "What you're smelling is sulfur; that's what it's mainly made of. If we can have it absorb some magnesium, it will explode. That's how we are going to get this."

So we all said, "How are we going to do this?"

He said, "Follow me."

As we head back into the school through the door we smashed, we head back to the swimming pool; "This, is where we are going to blow up the foam."

We said, "Really?"

He said, "Yes, go grab things for the foam to eat chairs, tables, etc. anything. It's slowing down because there is not a lot of stuff to eat, and hurry. Half of you do that, the other half stay here with me and let's set up our trap."

So, we get down into the pool, which has been empty for a while because they are painting the walls, so Mr. Roberson took the bucket of magnesium and sprinkled it all over the floor. He then said, "This paint is explosive. Open all the buckets and put it everywhere."

As we watched him take the rest of the magnesium and make a trail toward the bleachers, then, as we are leaving, he throws the rest of the magnesium all inside the pool, which was really crazy. After the other kids put the last of the chairs, desks, and other things they found, we all look at Mr.. Roberson, and he smiles for the first time.

"It's going to be a huge explosion, so make sure you kids are hiding. Now let's go get the foam and end this."

As we head into the hallway, we are very cautious, and we can see traces of where the foam went but couldn't find it. Just like that *bam!* It was in the auditorium, and it didn't take much to get it to chase us. We started running back to the locker rooms, and it was coming; it really wanted to consume us. As we head into the swimming pool area, it's right behind us. As we go to the left, Mr. Roberson heads to the right and takes his place behind the bleachers. The foam goes right by us and heads right in the pool, and man, it's huge! As it is consuming the tables, chairs, Mr. Roberson lights the magnesium, and we all hit the deck. Just then we hear Mr. Roberson say, "Oh shit." The magnesium stops igniting just before the edge of the swimming pool.

We were like, "Oh no." We then see Mr. Roberson go over to the edge of the swimming pool and try to light it, but he was too close, and the foam grabbed him, and we all yelled, "NO!" It was too late, and he went right in.

We then looked at each other and said, "We need to set that magnesium on fire." Just then one of the guys said, "Hold on, there are matches in the home ec room," so he goes, and when he gets back, Amanda grabs them. Mr. Roberson was her favorite teacher. She lights the whole pack and says, "This is for Mr. Roberson," and throws them in. We then grab her and hit the deck. *BOOM!!!!!!!!!!* It exploded so bad that it blew the back wall right out of the pool room. There was foam everywhere, all of it burned, and there was nothing left. We all stared down inside the pool and bowed our heads for the guy who saved all our lives, and maybe the whole community. After the school was rebuilt, they made a whole wing in the honor of Mr. Roberson for his love for science, his students, and the school he loved.

The End

Possession

I heard a bang and then the car started up all by itself. As it took off, I couldn't believe my eyes. That's what happened to me about ten years ago when I purchased this old car from this man on Craigslist. It all started when my car I was driving broke down, and the mechanic said, "It's going to need a new transmission." Ugh! That's too much money, so I started looking for a new car. I looked at a lot but couldn't find one in my price range, then I came across this one, a cherry 1969 Dodge Road Runner that looked great, so I contacted the owner and asked if I could look and drive the car, so we set up a time to meet, and I was a little apprehensive I didn't want to buy a junk, so I was cautious. When I got to his house, it was really run down and old. He came out with an oxygen tank in one hand and a cigarette in the other. He asked me what I was going to use the car for. I told him it would be my everyday driver. He likes that; he also told me that the car has feelings, you know.

I smiled like, "Yeah right."

He then said, "I won this car from a gypsy in Louisiana." He laughed, as he takes a drag from his cigarette then told me the whole story how he beat her in a card game, "She lost all her money, so I took her car to settle the debt. You know she was mad as hell." He laughs and almost chokes.

He opens the door to the garage and there sits this immaculate 1969 Dodge Road Runner Candy Apple red with white interior, and man, was this car looked sharp. I couldn't find anything wrong with it at first glance. He told me, "You have the same look I had thirty years ago. Isn't she a beauty?"

I was like, "Oh yes, yes, she is."

He then told me to back her out we will go for a ride. I sit behind the wheel, and man, this car is awesome. I start it up; it has this rumble. I look at him. He says, "Oh yeah, she's packing about eight hundred horsepower." He laughs and chokes again.

I back it out and into the sunlight. She shines so much it hurts my eyes to look at her. I said, "Mister, you can't be right about the price of this car. It's well worth more than you're asking."

He said, "Oh, it is, but I want the right person to own it."

We leave his house and turn on to the road. As we are cruising, he said, "Get on it." I smash the gas pedal and it just burns the tires until the smoke starts burning are eyes. We get cruising, and this car is amazing. It's an eye-catcher for sure, and it runs so nice. We pulled into his house, and he told me that the car is mine if I want it. I was overwhelmed and I couldn't get over it. I walked by the car and said, "You're mine, you sexy bitch."

Just then the old man said, "HEY, you don't talk like that to her. She doesn't like that."

I smiled and said, "What do you mean?"

He whispered in my ear that she's sensitive.

I was like, "What do you mean?"

He said, "If you do something to this car or hurt her feelings, she will let you know."

I was like, "Get out of here," and I laughed at him, and he said, "Be careful with her."

As I drove away, I was like, "Thanks, man, but I'll do what I want to her," and I smashed the gas pedal and left in a pile of smoke.

The next day, I was going to work with this beautiful car, and the weather was awesome, so I put the windows down and began listening to some music really loud, singing alone. I then went to turn the music up full blast, and that's as far as it went. I was like, "Damn, I can't even hear it." At the time, I never thought of anything of it and just lived with how high it went.

One afternoon, as I was going to following this slow car I was pissed about how slow the car was going. The next thing I know, the car speeds up, and we pass the slower car in a dangerous area, and we were going head on with another car in the opposite lane, I was screaming and trying to press the brakes, but the car wouldn't stop. I was like, "Oh shit," and just at the last minute, it swung back in the right lane, and it slowed down, and it was like nothing had happened.

I came on to the brakes and pulled into a small store, shut the car off, and got the hell out of it. Looked around and tried to see what or how this would have happened. I pressed the brake pedal as hard as I could, but nothing was happening, and the car wasn't stopping. After that scary ride, I brought it over to Gene's Auto Repair, my local mechanic, and asked him to check for an electric issue and the brakes. I came back that afternoon, and the car doesn't look like it has moved. I go in and say, "Hey, Gene. Did you get a chance to look at it?"

He said, "Yeah, but I couldn't start it. Do you have a kill switch on this car?"

I was like, "A kill switch? NO." I walk over and get inside, and it started right up.

Gene laughs. He said, "I tried to boost it and nothing. I'm way too busy right now to look at it, so you'll have to reschedule, pal, sorry."

So I leave Gene's, confused, and I start thinking of what happened last night. I reached down and grabbed the seat belt and pulled into the other lane on purpose to see what would happen, and the car didn't move a muscle. The wheel turns, but the car never moved. I was like, "What the hell is going on?"

Just then the seat belt started to get tight on me and I was having a hard time breathing. I then started to panic and then I said, "I'm sorry, girl. I won't do that again. Just as I said, that the belt loosened up, the radio came on, the windows went down, and we were listening to CCR's "Proud Mary"; the car was driving itself. I was so scared. We got home and I got out of that car ASAP! I then called the old man I bought it from, but his son answered the phone instead and told me that he was dying. I was so sorry. I asked his son if I could talk to him, since I am the kid who bought his car. The son said, "He has asked for you but we didn't know your name. Yes, please come over. He would like to see you."

I get there, and I park the car in the driveway and go in. The son said, "He hasn't got much time, just so you know."

I sit at his bed, and he looks terrible, hardly breathing. He asked me, "How's the car?"

I told him, "Okay," but I was lying. I hate that car.

He said, "I can see in your eyes that you know about her."

I shook my head.

He said, "Her name is Mary, and she's been alive for years, and if you don't mess with her, she will take good care of you, but you cross her, she will kill you!"

I was like, "How do I get rid of her?"

He looked at me and said, "You have to kill her. See, she knew I was dying, and I never drove her anymore. I had to sell her to break the cruise she put on me. I have had that curse on me for thirty years, and I am finally free." He smiled and said, "You must destroy her. That's the only way to free yourself from the car."

I was like, "I don't believe you." This was so overwhelming.

The old man yelled as loud as he could, "NO! NO! You must do it. If not, my boy, you see what has happened to me; it will happen to you! The only way to survive is to destroy the car and free Mary from it! There is no other way."

As the old man looked at me, he finally said "You have another alternative, my boy, just do it and you will be at peace."

The family then came in and they said, "He needs his rest. You must go now."

As I left the old man's house, I needed a plan, and it had to be sneaky because the car is very good at picking up on things. So that night, I played it cool and was whistling and everything like I was going out on the town, and I was like, "This is going to be one of the best nights ever."

As I was driving in the car, I had the music going and getting a little racy. The car was driving awesome, and it had no clue what was about to happen. I was pulling into the restaurant; my plan was already in process. See, what the car didn't know is that I told one of my friends whose dad had a salvage yard to bring over his flatbed, and I needed him to pick up the car and bring it over to his dad's crushing machine and mash it.

He was like, "Why? I thought you loved that car."

I then told him the whole story and what had happened; he then put the plan into action.

As I pulled up to the back of the wall and faced the car there, she wouldn't let me out. I think she knew something was up. I told her, "I am going in to get something to eat and see some of the boys." She then unlocked the car, and I left her there. I am waiting patiently inside and waiting for this to go down, but nothing.

Just then my friend calls me and said, "Hey, pal, why did you move your car?"

I said, "I didn't."

He then said, "It's right out front,"

I was like, "Damn, this isn't gonna go very well tonight, boys." She must be pissed, and now I'm done for. As I moved around the restaurant, she followed my every move. I knew I was in trouble. I then told my friend, "Is there a way you can block her from me and pick me up?"

He said, "Sure, I think we can do that." So he drove around the building, blocking her off from the door, then I had a bunch of people start a fake fight, so I could trick her into thinking I was involved in the fight. I then snuck out the back and got into his big tow truck.

I then hear the car come around the corner and come to a complete halt. It started to burn her tires. I knew she was pissed, so I told my buddy to go to the salvage yard. We pull in; she's right behind us but can't do a thing because the tow truck is so big. Just then we miss her, where did she go? We are looking around all over, and just then, she is flying in midair and lands right on the back of the tow truck as she tries to smash the cabin in. My buddy then heads over to the conveyor belt and picks up the bed and as she slides down on the bed. She's spinning her tires trying to escape, but no luck. Up the belt she goes and then gets tipped down into the crusher. It grinds her up, and you can hear weird things coming out of the machine-like squeals, it almost sounds like screams and then a huge puff of smoke, and that's it, As we watch the stuff go by us on the conveyor belt in small pieces, "It's over," I say to myself. I hope the old man feels free like I do. I then look at my buddy and I ask him, "Where does all the old, crushed-up metal go?"

As he walks away, he tells me, "Oh, they melt it down, and that's what all the new cars are made of…"

The End

Techo

Here in good old Nebraska, I lived with my mom and two older siblings in a quiet town just outside of the big city. My friends and I would play over at this old, abandoned Air Force base. All the fencing had been beaten up, and some of it was torn down, so it was easy to get into. It was a place a lot of kids went to hang out. I remember one sunny day, I told my friends, "Let's build a robot." They all laughed at me, but once I showed them the stuff we had there to do it, they had second thoughts. We started to work on the lower end first. We knew it had to have strong feet for maneuvering around all the obstacles on the base and some speed as well. We found just the thing on this old Cessna airplane. The lowering device was perfect: a small wheel which was made of this strong ten-ply rubber. We knew then we needed the next step up. I guess we were building it literally from the ground up. I was on to the stomach and midsection, and it was the hardest part to come up with. "We knew it had to be strong and be able to put things inside that will make it operate, but what? As we look around, we head inside the old air hanger. There is a lot of stuff inside here, like electronics and things like that. We start walking around, and we then head upstairs to the offices and the parts area, which is spread all the way back to the hanger wall.

As we were looking for whatever we thought a robot would need, I came across this huge box, and when I went to pull it out of the shelving, it was like, glowing .I thought it was just one of those lights that have a glow to them, but to my surprise, it was this electronic base plate that looked like it went on a print board or inside of a computer or something. When we picked it up. We were surprised; it had these two batteries that were hooked up to it. That's what the glow was. I have never seen a computer print board like this. We then went over to a robot and started to put it together.

Days go by and we all put in a lot of work building it, welding up the wheel, setting up the body, getting the hands all set up so they move around, and then it was time for the head. We really didn't think about what we were going to use. We then all started to go over the parts area again, hoping we would find something. Just then, one of my friends came across what looked like an old space helmet, with a shield intact. "That's it." We all agreed, and we then hurry up and start getting it fitted for the robot who still had no name. Hmm, what to call him?

Just then I said, "Hey, guys, we forgot to put the print board on the front side of his body."

"Oh yeah." We all laughed and then went to work doing that. After we were all done, it looked so cool, with those lights flashing and things blinking. We were all exhausted, so we left and said we would sleep on it and think about a name. We all agreed, and went home.

The next day, we get down to the hanger. We all look around for the robot, not sure what happened, why it wasn't there. We all looked at each other and were like, "Where is he?" We then started to split up and started looking for him.

Just then we heard a scream, and there was this robot that we all built rolling toward us! We all turned and started to run away, screaming out loud! It went flying by us and cut us off, then said, "Hi, boys!"

We all screamed again and started to run anywhere, but it was so fast. It then spun around us and made us push ourselves into a circle, and it was then standing right in front of us; we were mesmerized! It then went through and said hi to all of us. How does it know our names?

Just then I said in a soft voice, "How did you come to life?"

"I guess it was this power board. I'm not actually sure, but I feel awesome!"

We all laugh, and we then sit down and start asking him questions. He tells us everything about what we did to build him. "Each one of you built me, so that's how I know a little bit about you." It then said, "I want to explore," and we all yelled, "NO! You can't leave this place, do you understand?"

"Yes, yes, I see boys. Now who wants a ride on me!"

We all yelled, and one by one, we rode that robot around the entire hangar. That day was so much fun; we didn't want it to end.

"Just before leaving, we have to tell you something about outside of this hanger. "You see, people will come and take you, bad people."

He then said, "I don't compute."

We then explained to him what they would do if they found him.

He was silent for a second then said, "Okay, boys. I will stay here and wait for you guys to come back."

We then all looked around and said, "We haven't come up with a name for you." We looked at that print board and it had the name Technotronic Electronics on it; we looked at each other and then we all said, "Techno!"

Techno the Robot said, "I like that name, boys."

We all hugged him, and we left, closing the hanger door, and couldn't wait until tomorrow to have some more fun with him.

Days and weeks go by, having fun with Techno, going all over that hanger, which is huge, but we could tell Techno was sick of doing the same things over and over.

That night we all said bye to Techno, and as we watched him roll away, we could tell there was something wrong with him. We all agreed that tomorrow we were going to bring him outside and around the building. The next morning, we get to the hanger, and the door is open.

We were like, "Oh no!" We all yell for Techno, but nothing. We then notice his tracks as they go out of the hanger and head outside. We started to follow and noticed that he was going back and forth, like he was trying to escape someone or something. As we follow the tracks, it leads us to another hanger, just down a ways from the one we were at. As we start to go in, we hear someone yelling at us.

"HEY! Get away from that door!"

Just then we hear some noise coming from that hanger.

The guy then says, "What are you guys doing around here?"

We then all run away from him and head back to our hanger and close and this time lock the big door and all hide. Just then, we hear this guy coming toward our hanger; he stops his truck and gets out "Are you kids in here? You know you're on private property. I'll have you all arrested if you don't leave. You have until tonight."

He then walks back to his truck, and then he comes back to the door and kind of whispers, "I know what you're hiding in there, and it's going to be mine! I'll get it you, just wait. As he gets in his truck and drives away, here comes Techo, speeding around the corner, yelling to that guy, "Asshole, asshole!"

We all laugh, but now it's going to be an issue trying to hide Techno from this guy. We told him, "How did you get in?"

He said, "Follow me," and he told us of this huge hole way back in the hanger.

We were like, "How are we going to keep him safe?" We had no clue, and now this guy knows our secret. We were all running ideas around, and then I had a great idea.

I said, "What about the school?"

They all looked at me like I had three heads, but then they realized that school is out for the summer, and it would be a great place for Techno until we find another place for him. So, that night, we secretly snuck him in the school; it was hard because every place we went by he wanted to know who lived there and what their names were.

 As we leave the school, we tell him, "Don't roll around in the daylight, just at night, and no lights on close to the road." He agreed. We said, we will check on him later that night.

As we head to the hanger, we see big changes; it looks like they are replacing the old fence with a new one. We ask the guys who are doing the job.

They tell us that the whole property has been sold to one man, and they point over to him, and he notices us, and we start taking off through the woods. We get far enough away that he can't see us, but we hear him yelling, "This is my property now, boys, so stay off or I'll put all of you in jail!"

As he laughed walking away, "Now I'll take what's rightfully mine in that old hanger of yours."

We all look at each other and laugh, and we then start making our way to the school to see Techno.

As we get to the school, we see what looks like light that are being flicked on and off, UGH. We all head through the janitorial area to get in. We then head to the flickering lights in the back hallway. As we come around the corner, there's Techno, running back and forth, turning the lights on and off, we try not to laugh. We all yell at him, and he said, "Guys," as he speeds over to us.

We tell him the situation, and we say, "We may have to bring you to the old YMCA building, and you will have all the lower level of the huge building's basement to fly around, and you won't have to be bothered."

He agreed and we dressed him in this huge, long workman's coverall so you couldn't see his wheel, and we headed to the Y. We were all around him, so it was tough to see him, plus it was dark. As we head to the back of the Y, I thought that someone was following us, but I wasn't sure, so it then slipped my mind, and we get Techmo in there, and man, we played with him until it was time for us to go home. We all said, "We will see you tomorrow," and he said, "Later, dudes." He was a nut but we all loved that robot.

As we leave and I get home, I text the other guys and say I have a bad feeling about that place and the guys, some agree, some don't, so I told them, "Let's make sure we check on him tomorrow. It's Saturday, and maybe we can go and take him down the street again."

They all laughed. and that night we went to bed thinking everything was okay, but it wasn't!! Poor Techno, that lowlife guy on the base followed us that night and went in, and he didn't want Techno, just that print board, so he tricked Techno to go over to him, and he yanked it off him and then used a sledgehammer and pounded on him until he really beat him up.

That morning, I met everyone at our usual spot, and we were all excited to go over and see him, but when we got there, it was unreal. All the hard work to put him together, and he laid there in a pile of parts. I dropped to my knees and wept. I couldn't believe it. We all knew who was up to this, but how to get that board back? I had an idea, but we would have to trick that guy into giving us that board. "We all will have to work really hard to put Techno back together, we will use RC cars to make him move, and then we will make our very own print board out of Christmas lights and a metal box. Come on guys!! Who's in!"

We all yelled and started working on Techno; it took two to three days, and we had what looked like an awesome robot now to trick that guy and get the other print board back on Techno. We put our plan in motion and started going down the street right by the old base, trying to get this guy's attention, and man, did it work.

He came flying by the gate in his truck and said, "Hello, boys."

We all screamed and played right into the trap.

He said, "You have two of these robots, boys."

Just then one of the boys said, "Yes, this is the best one. It can do all kind of tricks."

We then told him to be quiet.

Just like that the guy said, "Oh, boys, I happen to come across another print board last night in the hanger while I was cleaning. Would you boys be interested in a trade?"

We said we might have to talk about it as a group.

Just then we saw one of the head security guards come over. He said, "Is there any issues over here, boys?"

We said, "No, sir. We are just making a deal with this gentleman."

The security guard then said, "I'll just stay here until the deal is done, so there is nothing going to happen." We then traded, and as we were leaving, we took off with makeup Techno and we headed to the Y.

We installed the print board, and Techno came to life again. It was amazing seeing him again flying through the Y's gym, happy as can be, and this time we were never going to leave him. What a summer that was, laughing, joking, and riding on Techno.

The End

The Bet

As we walked around this old, abandoned school I was thinking that maybe this wasn't the best of ideas. Just walking through the front door, we heard unexplainable noises and felt like we didn't belong there. First off, we lost a bet, and this was our punishment. It would be helpful to start from the beginning of this one.

One day at school, after history class with Mr. Bar, he started telling a group of us how many haunted houses were in our area. None of us could believe him that buildings in our town were haunted and we were being told by our teacher. After leaving class, the group of us got to thinking how we could make what Mr. Bar told us more interesting.

"What if we bet the Senior class that the juniors could outlast them at one of the haunted places Mr. Bar was talking about?" I asked the other guys.

"Tom, that is brilliant!" shouted Jared. Everyone started high-fiving as we made our way to the cafeteria to break the news to the Senior class president, Matt Stun.

As we walked into the cafeteria, approaching Matt's legendary popular circle table, conversation started to dissipate from the room.

"Matt, us Juniors have a little bet to place with you Seniors." Quincy started us off strong.

"What business would I have destroying some Juniors in a pointless bet that will humiliate them even more than they do to themselves?" Matt laughed, and his group echoed it. "On the other hand, why wouldn't I want to do that? Let's hear what you have, four eyes."

Quincy took a step back to let someone else take over, and in the moment all my nerves had left my body and I floated to the front and couldn't believe what I was doing.

"Juniors versus Seniors. Which class can last longer in the haunted, abandoned buildings of Jackson town?" I took a breath and let it sink in for the Seniors as smiles spread across their faces.

"Well, well, well. I didn't know we had haunted buildings in this shit town, but hey, the Senior class can't pass up an opportunity like this. What are the details, twerps?" Matt had an awfully dark look in his eyes, but we were exploding with confidence and didn't want to back down.

"The place is the old Jackson Town High School. It's been abandoned for thirty years, and rumor has it, that it's haunted," explained Jared. "Twenty-four hours is the length of the bet. Whichever class has the most people left at the end of the time wins the bet. During these twenty-four hours, each class will be exploring the school and trying to outlast the others. Sound like something you're up for?" Jared smiled and waited for the Seniors to respond.

"Well, if you all are ready to get your asses kicked, then sure. Let's make this happen." Matt smirked and thrust his hand out for Jared to shake on it. "Let's make things a bit more interesting. If you're up for it, we meet at the school tonight at eight P.M." We all looked at each other, trying to gauge agreement, and knew we wouldn't want it any other way.

"Deal." Jared shook Matt's hand, and we all celebrated as we prepared for the bet of our lives.

I didn't initially know what we got ourselves into, but it became pretty clear as we walked through the front doors of the abandoned Jackson Town High School. Well, as we broke through the boarded up-front doors of the school, things were hard from the beginning. Saying it looked run down was an understatement. With paint peeling and ceiling tiles hanging by threads, this school would give us all a run for our money.

"All right, Seniors. Here we are. Now any ground rules you'd like to set or shall we start the clock?" Jared winked at the girls the Seniors brought.

"None on our end. I guess we'll see you all around the school, and hopefully, your mommies don't start worrying and you'll get called back home." Steve, one of the bigger football players, started to make baby noises as us. We shook our heads and watched as the twelve Seniors took a left and headed toward the east side of the building.

We started by heading down the hallway to the northside of the school and ended up finding the gym a little ways down the hall. We decided to keep moving but were stopped dead in our tracks when we heard what we thought was a basketball bouncing in the gym.

"What the hell was that?" Quincy whispered under his breath. We walked slowly back to the gym when the noise stopped. As we peered into the gym, we didn't see anything other than debris and broken floorboards. The minute we turned our backs, we heard the basketball again and started to run toward the front entrance where we started at.

"What the HELL was that?" We were all freaking out and we hadn't even made it all the way down the first hallway.

"We have to get a grip, guys. What if we group up and see what we can find? We brought the walkies, right?" I asked the group. At least one of us needed to stay calm in the moment.

"Yeah, that sounds good to us," Jared responded, and the others nodded. We split up into two groups, each taking a walkie and enough courage to last the next twenty-four hours.

Group one went toward the west end hallway that looks like it leads towards the swimming pool area. Group two, my group, headed toward the north again toward what used to be the shop classrooms.

As we were walking, we stayed tight together, and even though we had each other, it felt terrifying. We moved slowly past the shop doors, and when one slammed shut after we walked by, we couldn't control our fear.

"What was that?" I whispered to the others. No one dared to answer, but we moved on. After a few minutes of waiting for someone to jump out at us, group two walked to us and said they were not enjoying this bet at all. They could hear footsteps behind them and people whispering, but there was never anyone there when they looked. We all knew it was going to be a long night.

As our group entered the swimming pool area, we all had a weird feeling about it. We heard a scream cut through the silence as one of our friends, Martha, dropped to the ground.

"Martha! What is it?" We all crowded around her.

"I saw something. There was a shadow that just moved across the pool." She was shaking as she told us, and we didn't waste any more time. We grabbed her off the floor and got out of the pool area as fast as we could. Just past the doors and back in the hallway, we heard a voice through the walkie.

"Freaky stuff is happening over here, guys," Zander whispered through the walkie-.

"What's going on, man? Shit is going on here too," Jared responded on our end.

"We were heading through some doors near the classrooms to the east of the gym when a door shut behind us. We had to run through a bunch of side rooms to escape whatever it was." Zander was whispering still, and we could hear the panic in his voice. "We got so twisted around, we have no idea where we ended up, but a lot of us are crouching in the corner of the machine room. We got in here, and I'm not kidding, we saw some type of figure float across the floor and through the wall! Not even a minute after the lights started turning on and off."

"Shit! Zander, Martha thought she saw a figure in the pool area." We all nodded. "You should follow it. Maybe it is trying to tell us something!" Jared told Zander.

"Well, everyone here seems to like that idea, so we'll give it a try. Keep the Walkie volume up on your end in case we have any troubles. Over and out." Zander cut off from the line and we decided to keep moving.

We decided to stay close to the pool area in case we saw anything like Martha did. We looped around and around until we came to the entrance to the women's locker room. We heard something, and everyone just looked at one another and shrugged. As we continued to walk closer to the sound, we couldn't believe what we were hearing; it was the shower running! Just as we turned the corner to the showers, the water stopped, and we walked into a silent shower with a wet floor.

"None of this makes sense," whispered Martha. "How is the water still running in an abandoned school this old?" It was the perfect question for what we were about to hear next; none of us were ready.

We moved through the locker rooms and were feet away from the pool entrance, when we all heard an unmistakable splash coming from a pool that has been empty for thirty-plus years.

We all stood in shock, not knowing if we should investigate or get the hell out of there. We slowly made our way back to the pool, glancing into the empty hole where it would be impossible to hear a splash.

"I feel like we are getting pranked so hard right now. How did that even happen?" Quincy shook his head, and we all echoed his worry and fear.

We started to move toward the school wings with old, tattered signs saying we were getting closer to the library. Just as we were turning a corner near the entrance to the library, we were halted in our tracks as we looked at an apparition of what seemed to be a janitor mopping the floor in front of us.

"Do you all see that?" Jenny asked. We all nodded, and before we had a chance to act, the janitor looked up and disappeared right in front of our eyes.

The girls in our group screamed and ran for the entrance of the library. We knew things were just going to get worse at this point. We followed them into the library, blocked up the doors, and took a second to catch our breath. As we were talking about what was happening, we caught Zander on the walkie.

"Hey, G2, just wanted to give an update. We followed the ghost thing out into the hallway, but it said nothing. We're walking toward the Home ec room because there is this amazing smell coming from one of the kitchens. We can't resist! We'll keep you updated. Over and out." Zander and his group seem to have stumbled upon the Seniors, but we were wrong to assume that.

They reached the kitchen to find it completely gutted, no stoves, ovens, fridges; it was completely empty.

"What the hell?" Zander and the others moved between the rooms, still smelling and unbelievably wonderfully blueberry scent, only to find more rubble and debris after every turn.

"We should get out of here; this is creeping me out." The group agreed, and they started to set out to find the others.

We all thought the library would be the place to be, but it was gutted, just like everywhere else. All the books were gone and only a few shelving units remained intact. A VCR machine sat near the circulation desk, so they went over to see if it was still connected. The cords had been destroyed and the inside had been taken, so they got comfortable at a small table and waited for any news from the other group. Within minutes, they heard what seemed to be a machine running and then *Old Yeller* showed up playing on the wall from the VCR machine they thought was destroyed.

The group screamed and made their way out of the library as fast as they could, heading toward the D wing of the school, not in any path of the other group trying to find them.

We stopped running when we heard the other group's screams and started to head back toward the library. We pushed open the doors to get to the next wing and with a huge bang, they closed behind us.

"Jared, try the doors. I really think we went the wrong way." I started to panic a little bit. Jared kept trying the doors, throwing his body against them with no give.

"They're locked. Shit." We all started to pace around until we saw people running toward us through the doors; it was the other group!

We were waving and smiling, glad to see the other group was safe. Zander picked up his walkie and motioned for us to do the same.

"How did the doors get locked? We have to get out; we only have an hour or so left." Zander seemed concerned we wouldn't be able to get out to win the bet.

"We ran through the doors to try to find you, but they locked after we got through them." We all nodded to them.

"Let's send two from each side to walk down the hall like twenty feet or so to see if there is a way for us to join groups. We have to rush."

We send Jared and Quincy. Zander sends Nathan and Missy. The two come back from both groups and tell us they can't see any paths to connect.

"Well, now what are we supposed to do?" Missy asked. Just then, a huge bang interrupted the groups, and they both decided in the moment to run for it.

My group headed back the way they came, down the long hallway pass the library. We noticed the door open to the music room, so we head in to see if we can find a way to get to the other group. Meanwhile, Zander and his group headed the other way up and around the corner in the C wing. Once they made it to the end of the hallway, they saw a door that seemed to lead out of that wing, but it was locked.

Zander couldn't stand being there any longer, so he found a chair and smashed out the window. He helped get the others out of the school where they came face to face with all of the Seniors.

"Well, well, well. I guess the Seniors couldn't last as long as they thought they could," Zander taunted Matt. He knew that our group had to make it out before the time was up, so they took a seat on the front steps and prayed we would find our way out in time.

"Tom, Jared! The Seniors are out here; we won if you can get out of here in time. I hope you get this message, just keep fighting!"

I smiled as Jared, and I and the others looked down at the walkie we really needed to get out so we could finally settle this bet. We split up in the music room, looking for a door to be unlocked so we could get out of there.

"Over here! This one is unlocked!" Martha screamed for us to follow and before we knew it, we were back on the main side of the school making our way through the woodshop area near the gym. We ran through the hallway, past the gym, and through the front doors to cheering fellow Juniors and a group of irritated Seniors. We laughed and cheered with each other knowing we could last longer than the others. Could you?

The End

The Cedar Field

As the verdict came down in the courtroom, some of the crowd sighed, some cheered, and then the prisoner listened to the judge who gave him his sentence. He told the young man first-degree murder is a very serious crime in this time and age; he then told him to stand up, and he then was explaining what the laws were for his crime. See, in 3031 there aren't a lot of prisons, the prisoners go to The Cedar Field, and then he told him, "You are guilty of first-degree murder of a young child. God bless you, young man, you have been condemned to The Cedar Field!"

The crowd screamed, some clapped, his family were hysterically crying and screaming at the judge, and then the officers took him away. The Cedar Field!! It's a one-hundred-acre property with a twenty-five-foot electric fence all around it. You see, prisoners are given seventy-two hours to get from one side to the other; if they make it, they are put in a holding home center, kind of like a medium-level prison per say, but that's the problem; it's set up for failure. They never had anyone make it from one end to the other; it hasn't happened in the seventy-five years of being introduced. Outside people have no clue, but inside the property are other things like animal traps and even snipers. It is the worst thing ever because no one has ever made it; it's designed to rid the population of the violence in the world.

The next day, they release the kid in the front gate of the Cedar Field; he is given this bracelet that measures his heartbeat plus, it lets the Correctional Facility know where he is.

He is given a small sack of food and he's off. The kid starts off pretty strong, then he must have got disoriented, and then watching the heart monitor that was when we heard a scream, and then nothing; the monitor goes dead, and just like that the young man is dead as well; he never had a chance. The Cedar Field claims another one; it's just the way it's set up.

As this is going on, another murder happens in this city; it's a rough neighborhood. They bring this guy in the courtroom, a rough-looking man who is ripped and is huge six-four or six-five, 270 pounds of a man. He just stood there and didn't say a word.

The Judge says, "How do you plea, mister?"

He then said, "Not guilty."

The Judge then said, "Well, you did kill a man with your bare hands."

He said, "It was in self-defense, sir."

"Well, the court will decide on that, son." The judge then asked, "What's your name?"

He said, 'You can call me Stone."

"Well, Mr. Stone, it doesn't seem you have ever been in trouble before. It seems we can't even find anything about you, Mr. Stone."

"Well, you see, Your Honor, I was a military guy, and the stuff I did was top secret, so that is why you can't find me in your system."

"That doesn't matter in my court, son, what you did in the military. I decide the law here, you understand, son?"

"Yes, sir."

"Take him below. We will try him tomorrow, and Mr. Stone, if you try something with my boys here, I'll hang you! You understand that, son?"

"Yes, sir."

"Smart answer. Now bring him downstairs."

As they are walking him down, one of the officers says to the other one, "Look, boys, we have a top-secret military guy here, hahahahaha." They all laugh at him and then that officer struck Stone right in the side of the face with his baton, and then Stone stood up and face-smashed that guy, kicked the other two, and then he ended up walking himself down to his cell, where another officer was there waiting who took the cuffs off and put him in his cell.

Twenty minutes later, the judge walked down to Mr. Stone's cell and said, "I told you to behave yourself, Stone."

"Look at my face. One of your officers hit me. What do you think I was going to do?"

"Guess what, Stone. You don't get a trial, you're condemned to The Cedar Field."

Stone lunges at the judge and grabs him by the neck and slams him into the bars and says, "I'll be back for you; you're dead!"

The officers then Taze him but he doesn't let go down, and they do it again and again and he finally lets go and hits the floor.

The next day, they feed him, but they put something in his food, and after he wakes up, he was at the front of the fence as they threw water on him to wake him.. As he got to his feet, there were about fifteen guns on him and knew where to go. One of the officers carries a large tablet and on; it's the judge. He says, 'Good morning. Mr. Stone. As you know from your actions yesterday, we have moved ahead on your trial and I have come to terms that your guilty and the verdict is The Cedar Field

He went to say something, and the judge yelled over him, "You're done, my boy. Can't handle the way the world is today, so I condemn you to the Field. God bless you. May he help you on your way."

Just then Stone kicked the officer in the face and grabbed the tablet and said, "I'm coming for you!" Then one officer hit him in the head, and they grabbed his arm to put the bracelet on, but he jumped up and headed into the field. One looked at the other and they said, "Shit, this isn't going to go over too well." They closed the door and called over to the head office and told them; they weren't too upset but now how to see where he is, that's what's going to be a challenge. As Stone is walking into the field, he sees a trail but doesn't go on it; he starts to think about how the jungles were and how they trapped people, so he stays off the trails, looking for whatever he can for shelter and maybe some food. He makes his way close to this opening and stays hiding in the thick brush and waits there for a while. He then notices this one guy who popped his head up like he heard something. Stone knows that might be one of the snipers, so, very carefully, he makes it close to him jumps on his back and overtakes the guy.

He then undresses the guy, takes his gun and radio. The guy had some food and water, so he takes that as well and goes back in the tall brush to wait around for whatever would walk by. It's dark now, so he starts moving again, staying off the trails and looking for other people, and he finds another sniper in a tree. Stone takes out the night-vision goggles and holds up his rifle and takes that guy out. He moves on and figures he's about three quarters of the way across the field. Just then he hears a growl; he turns, and it's a huge Bobcat. It jumps at him, but he takes his knife and stabs it while it's in the air and ends the cat's life. He moves on, only to get caught in one of the field's traps. He fell into a hole with sharp sticks and just sliced a little of his leg, but he did yell out, so that got some attention over where he was. Just like that, he heard a couple bullets that flew over his head as he lay really still, trying to control the bleeding. As he made it to the thick cedar bushes, he propped up his rifle and took out that sniper and one more as he moved closer to the end of the property. As he looks through the brush, he sees the gate of freedom, but it has some work to do; he remembers that he has the uniform of the guy he took off earlier. Stone then comes up with a plan; he walks out and yells for help. Two of the three officers come to this side; he shoots them and then heads for the last guy at the gate. Stone dives under some brush, and they begin in a shooting battle that Stone wins. He is now safe to walk out of that place. First thing, he tapes up his leg and takes a car that's there and heads over to the courtroom. He parks it and starts walking up the stairs. Some of the officers there ask him, "Who are you?" He shoots them and starts to look for the judge. The warning alarms go off, and just then, way down the hallway he sees the judge and starts shooting at the group surrounding him. They return fire and people are falling all over, and Stone notices the judge holds his chest, and down to the floor he goes. Stone then knows his job is complete. Stone then hides behind a big pillar and starts to make his way back to The Cedar Field. He drives around front and shoots the control box that opens the doors, then he drives in the back entrance and closes the door behind him He then shoots the control box and drives deep into The Cedar Field, where he stops for a bit to rest and looks around. He then realizes this is the place that he wanted all along, where he will spend the rest of his life, free.

The End

The Gulf

The place is called The Gulf; it's a piece of property right up on the Canadian border, kind of like a marsh and wet; a lot of things have happened up there that no one can answer and even tell you how it happened. See, it's haunted; it has been for years. People have went missing up in there and never to be seen again. It's not because they can't find their way back, it's just like they never had a chance to. Rumor has it there is a crazy animal roaming the place; it eats whatever it wants. Some say they have seen it from a distance and it's ten feet tall and huge, and hairy and about six hundred pounds or more. It walks really slow, but they say it can fly from tree to tree. My grandpa told me one day he heard a rumor that a couple of scientists went up with a group of kids from college to do some research on the property to find out if some of the myths are true or not. He remembers because of all the chaos around the town that evening.

He tells me that the group headed up the Cannon Corners Road toward the Gulf. Just as they arrive, a farmer, Mr. DeCause, was out front of the entrance and asked them what they were going to do. The professor told him what they wanted to do, and the farmer told them that this was bad. He told the professor, "I lose cattle up there. I don't ask questions, and I don't pry or push the thing, whatever it is. It's evil and mean and doesn't care about anything." The professor told the farmer we are not staying the night, we are leaving early. The farmer yells at him; all the students look. He said, "You'll be sorry. You're crazy to go up there, you go and you'll never come back!"

Some of the kids then said, "Is this such a good idea to go up there?"

The professor said, "Don't listen to him, he has no idea, and that was just a rumor; there is nothing up there for us to be scared of." So the vans started to head to the Gulf. As they proceeded to drive into the bush, the kids noticed that there weren't a lot of birds chirping or any little animals like squirrels and chipmunks running around. It was a little scary looking. Then they made it to the parking spot; the rest of the way they had to walk to get to the area called the Gulf. As they gathered all the stuff, everyone was on edge and the professor said, "Let's just stick together and make sure we all look around and watch each other." The kids didn't know but the professor was carrying a handgun, and he also didn't feel so great at this place.

As they made it to the flat rocks, the kids saw the giant opening, rock ledge on both sides and about twenty-five feet across, then twenty feet down to very dark water.

"This is The Gulf," said the professor. "In the prohibition years, they used to jump this with cars to get into Canada from the US."

One of the students said, "What's down in the water?"

The professor said, "Everything you can think of, cars, money, weapons, people."

They said, "People?"

He said, "Maybe, remember It's twenty-five feet across some cars didn't make it. When prohibition was active, you didn't want to get caught, so they tried to jump the opening to get into Canada, If you made it, great; if you didn't, in there you ended up," as he pointed to the deep, dark water.

As they turned away one student asked him how deep it was. He said, "A hundred feet or more. No one knows really how deep it really is." Then the professor said, "Okay, let's split up into three groups. Remember, we all have whistles."

They all said yes,

He then said, "Do not go anywhere without a partner, does everyone understand? It's thick bush out here and we don't want anyone to come up missing."

With that said, the groups of three, with five in each group began to go and explore The Gulf; each group had things that they were looking for. Group one was with the professor, and they were looking for any strange-looking small animals; group two were the seniors, and they were looking for strange plants, and group three, they were the lower classmen and they were checking the land out and how The Gulf became. It was getting toward the early afternoon when we, group three, heard this strange sound coming from over near the farmer's property.

We stopped and looked at each other and it was like, "What the hell was that?" We never heard that again and was wondering if the other groups heard that. As we keep researching, we find ourselves migrating toward the sound we all were interested in and what that sound was. Group one was toward the road that we came in on, and they didn't hear any of that. They were on the move, looking for small animal tracks. Group two was right in the middle of the noise; they all looked at each other and were like, "What the hell was that?" They couldn't figure out what it was.

Just then a loud noise came across the group, who was in a kind of straight line, and everyone looked forward, and just like that three of the members were taken. After looking forward at the noise, the other two looked back and all they saw were two backpacks, nothing else. They started to freak and blow their whistles, but being so nervous and scared, they couldn't, so then they started running; the problem was they were running the wrong way; instead of towards the others, they were heading deeper into the woods. Group three found themselves almost in the back of the farmer's property. They couldn't get over how fast they got confused and how much they had walked but knew they needed to find a way back, so they thought going to the farmer's house, he could help them get back.

As they walked around the side of the house, one of the students said, "This feels all wrong," but the other ones said, "We are just asking for help, that's it." But as they came around the front of the farmhouse, the outside garage door was locked, so three students stayed there and two went along the other side to see if they could get in.

Just then they hear this god-awful roar, then they all look at each other and are freaked out. "Let's go get the others and get the hell out of here." As they come around the corner no one is there, just their backpacks; they then are like, "What's going on here?" They grab their bags and head out toward the road, yelling. Group one is with the professor and they find themselves wandering down a dirt road and lost. Just then in the distance they see the farmer on his tractor, it's his hired hand; he stopped to ask if everything is okay and the professor says, "Well, we are a little lost."

He tells them that they are a ways away from the vans, so the professor has two students ride on the back of the tractor to go and bring back the van for them. They leave and then the rest get back to work looking for small animals. Meanwhile group two started to head back to the vans but was so disoriented that they were heading towards the professor's group. After a while they met up and had to tell the professor what was going on and that they couldn't find two of their friends. The professor was like, "This trip is a disaster. Okay, let's start heading back to the vans, where the other two are that went with the farmer's hired hand. Okay, let's stay together."

As they make it to the vans they see group three and they also tell the professor that they are missing two of their friends. Also, the professor is like, "What is happening here?" He then tells most of them to stay at the vans and not go anywhere; they all agree, and he takes three of the boys and they go in toward the Gulf to find the others.

As they walk in they hear this loud scream what sounds like a person screaming, so they go towards the scream. As they get to where we think that it came from, nothing, but then one of the students said, "Look at these drag marks." They follow the drag marks, and it gets them to this cave like opening; they go inside and find all the kids that are missing.

The professor is like, "What's going on here?"

The kids are stuck to the side wall of the cave with this sticky glue over their mouths. I told the other students to try and get these kids down, one of them removed the glue gunk on the kids' mouth He started panicking, "GET ME DOWN! HE'S COMING BACK!"

We told him to keep quiet, "and who is coming back?"

He was squirming, trying to get down. "The monster." We all looked at each other, and then he said, "He comes in and checks on us all the time. It's huge and it looks like a Sasquatch, that's all I know. Man, it's like ten feet tall! Hurry up and get us down."

"What's this stuff that has you stuck like glue?"

"Yeah, I don't know; he makes it over there in that rock bowl."

We started to release one of them and we then heard that scream again. The student said, "HIDE! He's coming back; put that on my face again, and you guys better hide somewhere or you're done."

So we started to head farther back in the cave and behind some rocks. We then waited to see this huge creature. He starts to walk in and all I can see is his huge upper body. I was in awe; it was a huge Sasquatch, eight maybe nine or nineteen feet tall, massive frame, and he was looking around. He then brought a half of a deer carcass over to eat. He never once looked up at the kids or anything; it was unreal. Just then we heard what sounded like a helicopter. He took off, heading right for us. We froze behind the rock, and he ran behind us, and as we listened, he kept going, then we saw this light at the end of the cave. I stood up and said, "Let's go get these kids down. This is our only shot at it."

So as we get the last one down and are leaving, the helicopter is circling around again, and we see it's the CBP Homeland Security, checking the border I guess, but we were so thankful for that. As we were heading back to school, we couldn't believe what had happened. I asked the students what had happened to them. They couldn't remember anything; their memories are cloudy; physically, they weren't hurt, but mentally, they are scared. It was an unreal trip where friends and families won't believe us.

A week after, we all meet up to go over things about our trip and how the kids are dealing and if we can help them. We all get in a circle, and I start by saying, "I have dreams about that cave. Does anyone else?" They all raise their hands.

One of the students got up and handed her phone to me; she was one of the ones that got taken. She speaks and says, "I walked around the side of the house to see if the side door was open, and I was videoing as I walked around, and not sure I got this or what happened but…" I open up her phone and there she is, walking alongside the house talking and shooting the video, then you see this huge hand full of hair come across her. She then falls, and the phone hits the ground, and then a couple minutes go by. You see that huge hand grab the phone, turn it, and then…what we saw was unbelievable: the face of an animal…SASQUATCH. All our heads dropped, then the phone went dead. She said, "That's all I have." She showed us the original phone, which was squeezed so tightly it was hard to get the sim card out, but we did and this is what we have. I don't know how we got to the cave or how we were knocked out. I just know I never want to go through that again. As we sit in a circle and talk about what happened, we all come to an agreement that we are never going to talk about it again or bring it up.

The End

The House

Hanging out at my friend's house watching TV, when I asked him, "What else is on? This show sucks."

He said, "Let's watch a scary movie on the DISH."

I was like, "Hell yeah, that would be better than what we were watching."

So as we get into this Dracula show, it goes to a commercial, and this game show comes on called *The House*, a reality TV program that's real. You enter the house and have forty-eight hours to get out; you also have to deal with situations through the whole house, and to win, you have to survive. I told my buddy, "You wouldn't last in there, pal"; he said the same for me, and I then told him, "Let's enter."

"No way, man. I'm not doing that, plus you have to do it on your cell phone. "There is no trick about it that's how you enter, and he had a dinosaur for a phone, Haha.

So I answer the qualifying questions and I'm put on a list. So I tell him "When's the next show air?"

"Tuesday," he said.

I was like, "Great, I'll be back to watch."

He laughs. "You're crazy to do that."

"You know you actually don't die, they are just removing you from the house when you fail to pass through the stations."

He said, "I hope so for your sake, pal."

So Tuesday comes around and we watch *The House*; it's a little corny; you start with eight players, but once one goes, it seems that they all start dropping out; when they enter the house. It's pretty unreal, and it really looks real as shit. As the group walks into the house, the floor opens up and right off, two are fall into a pit with sticks in it. They show those kids real quick and they look dead to me. I was like, "Damn, that's nasty." Then they head to the kitchen, and knives are thrown at them one more time. It's really a massacre for these kids. Plus, you don't have to follow anyone. You can go your own way and whoever finishes it is the winner. As I watch in my head, I would do different things than these guys, plus you really can't have a partner so it's all you. We watch for the whole hour, and one guy gets real close, but just as he is heading to an open window, he puts his head into the window, and it comes down right on his head; he's done.

I tell my buddy, "This is nuts. Why would you do that? It was so predictable."

He said, "What would you have done?" and I told him, "The opposite, that's for sure; it's too easy, you have to do the totally opposite in that show." So I tell him, "I'll see you next Tuesday to watch it again because I don't get that show on cable."

So Tuesday rolls around and we watch the next episode, and it's the same old thing; this time I'm yelling at the TV for the people to move or don't go in there, but once again it's the same ol' thing, they all die. At the end of the show they are going to call the next group, and as I tell my buddy I'll see you later, I leave, and he's yelling at me, "Hey, man, they just called your name."

I was like, 'Yeah right. Stop messing with me, pal."

He said, "They did."

Just then I get an email. Sure enough, "Call this number if you're still interested in being on the show." I called immediately and say "I'm in."

They said, "We will see you in the afternoon just before the show goes on," and they gave me instructions how to get to the place. I was so excited. I called my buddy and asked him if he wanted to come with me. Of course he said yes, and we headed right over.

As we get there, it's unreal; there are people everywhere, and they are only letting one person on the set and if your name is on a list. We park the car, and over in the distance we see a hearse I was like, "What the hell is that here for?" and then something of fear came over me as we walked up the set, and man, did it look creepy in real life.

As we find the director, he has me go into this room with the other guests and he said he would be in a bit to go over the rules. I was like, "Okay, no problem." I walk in, and there are a variety of different types of people, a big strong guy, what looks like two CrossFit people, I know those type, shocks all the way up to their knee and a headband on, lol, then what looks like a really smart guy, myself, and two other girls that look scared as hell.

Just then the door opens and in comes the director and what looks like his muscle and a lawyer I would say, and he goes over the rules and how things go. First, he tells us all this game is real; everyone looks at each other, and one of the girls ask if the people on TV really die. He takes a bit and says yes, they did. "That why you must sign this waiver to play; if you don't you will be escorted off the property and someone else will get the money. Remember you are playing for two million dollars."

I ask if anyone has ever won yet; he said, "Nope but we have had some people come close."

I said under my breath, "And now they are dead."

He heard me and said, "Not everyone dies, some do, but man, it's two million bucks! So who's in?"

We all looked at each other and I was the last one to sign. "Good. Do what you need to get ready. We start in fifteen."

I was so nervous, but I watched the other shows and what not to do, I am going to do the totally opposite. I guess that was my plan. One of the girls that looked scared came over to me and said, you're not stretching."

I was like, "We aren't running a marathon. It's all up here," as I point to my head, "and that's what I'm stretching"; as everyone else who was stretching stopped, I smiled. The director comes in and says, "Good luck, everyone, you're going to need it."

I was the last one to leave the room, and I asked his muscles softly if anyone ever won; he shook his head no, then he said, "That's the point, there will never be a winner," and he laughs while walking away. I had a lot of doubts, but I had a plan, and that's what I'm sticking with: slow and steady wins the race.

Just as we start and enter the house, it's typical, everyone starts to follow the big strong guy. I was like, "Nope, I'm doing my own thing."

He then said to me, "Hahahaha, you're going to die."

I looked at him, "Wanna bet, bud?" and that's the last I saw of him as they went straight. I went to the left, and I was heading into what looked like a library, and *Here we go*, I told myself.

Just then I heard screams, but I don't move the house has traps and hidden rooms everywhere. I can only assume something happened to that group. I was all by myself and liked it that way.

As I moved really slow in the library, the floor started to move up and down; my first response was to hold on to something, but remember, I'm doing the opposite, so I stay in the middle of the floor and ride out the movement, and right to the left of me the chair where I was dropped right into the basement, I assume, and if I was holding on to that I would have been gone-zo. I move a bit more, and out of the closet there is a hallway, and to the right of the hallway is a set of stairs, so I take the stairs just to get off the first floor, still no sign of the others, and man, it's black like the night in here. Small steps up the stairs, and it's a huge staircase, so I hug the wall and go up very slowly. I hear something coming; it's picking up pace, and man, it sounds like it's moving quickly; just then, I see a shiny thing coming down the stairs. I push up against the wall, and just then, it goes flying by me, just rubbing my shirt; it looks like a metalhead but, man, it takes out half the stairs on the way down. I go a little farther and see up ahead a flat resting place. Just as I take the step to get on it, the stairs go flat! I reach up and grab the rug that's on the floor, and that saves me from falling all the way down the stairs, and once I am up, the stairs go back. I shake my head. This is so tough. I sit in this chair but then was like *Shit*, and it moves back, and I find myself sliding down this ramp into what looks like a laundry shoot, and at the end is one of the two girls who were scared and she breaks my fall, and I jump back and I am asking her if she is okay, but she never moves. I grab her hand, and no pulse. Oh man!! She's dead. I almost lose it, but I controlled myself and tried to move her, but I couldn't. Why? I pull on her again, and then I see why; she landed on a huge stake, which impaled her. I feel bad, that's the first person I have seen dead; now to get out of here. As I walk around the basement, there's not a lot of options to get out, just the stairs, so I start to climb up very slowly, and I get to the top, but the door is stuck, so I give it a little push, and nothing. Just as I go to really push it, I wait a second, and it opens right up and right across the way is a window. I would have went right through it if I pushed hard enough. Oh lord.

Well, at least I am back in the upper level of the house. Where is everyone? I walk toward two swinging doors and enter what looks like the dining room, and oh boy, what a sight. There is the muscle guy stuck to the wall. It looks like he stepped on something and it tripped a huge trap door from the ceiling with sharp, pointy metal rods that sent him against the wall and impaled him. I went over to see how he was, and nope, he's dead. This game is starting to really sink in that one wrong move and you're not going home, plus this house is huge and I have no clue where I am. I stop for a second to find my bearings, and I hear voices I yell, "Hey, I'm over here," and then a voice came back, "Hahaha, you're going to die, hahaha." It sent chills down my spine, and I kept moving very slowly through the dining room and it leads me out into a long-ass hallway with a lot of pictures on the wall. I remember this in the first episode; the floor gives out just up ahead. I walk very slow through it, but nothing. I walk almost to the end, and I was like, "This can't be right."

Just then where I was standing it drops out and the only thing I can grab is the lamp on the wall. I'm hanging there, and I look down; two more people, the Cross Fitters, landed into a pit of what looks like snakes. DAMN! I close my eyes and I pray this lamp holds me. The floor, then flips up again, and I touch it really softly; it's hard, and I run out into the hallway, and as I turn quickly I'm in the kitchen, and I hear something coming, whistling. Just then I see a set of knives coming at me. I hit the floor, but one gets me right in the right arm. OUCH, it burns; it's not too deep but enough to have the thing bleed all over, so I rip a piece of my shirt and tie it around the cut. I then try to get through the kitchen without having any other troubles, but the floor is so slippery, it's tough to stand, and I am wondering why. Well, I found out just then. I'm near the sink, and it feels like the floor is lifting up and the table and all the kitchen pots and pans are heading right toward the other end of the kitchen, right where the stove is, and oh, by the way, it's now on and flames are coming out of it. This house is unreal. It's so hard to give up but what keeps me going is that huge amount of money. As I smile, I hold on tight to the sink until it is over, then I move on to the next room/station. I haven't seen anyone for a while now.

Where is everyone? I'm now heading into what looks like the parlor. This house is huge; how many more rooms, and what's my time? I have no idea. I keep moving on. This room the ceiling seems really low as I walk a little faster it seems to be moving down on top of me and I am starting to panic because I need to get to the other end and I begin to run almost a full sprint. Just then I hit this wall of plexiglass that looks like a mirror, and I don't remember anything else. I don't know how long I was out, but it must have been awhile. As I lay there, I hear talking, and it's one of the geeks and one of the twins and myself, that's it. As I try it get up, the room is like a couple inches away from my face and I can't move; the only thing I can think is if someone comes in, it will release a switch to get me out of here. I can't yell or speak. It's too hard to move my chest. This sucks. I don't want to lose this way. I worked so hard; we are almost done.

Just then I heard footsteps and once whoever entered the ceiling started to rise up once I got air in my lungs I yelled, "DON'T MOVE!" I ran back to them and was at the entrance of the parlor; they looked at me and said, "Damn, you look like shit."

The skinny girl said, "You know we have to get through this room."

I said, "Yeah, I know, but unless you have a plan it's not happening, it's the hardest room to enter."

"What happened to you? Why is your face all bloody and your eyes swollen?"

I told them about the ceiling, and when I started running, I ran into this plexiglass and they were like, "Wow, let's do this room at the end. Do you guys want to stay together until the end?"

We all agreed, we would stay together until the end and split the money, we left that room and headed down this small hallway toward what looked like a washer/dryer room, which was huge and smelly. As we walk into the room, it seems to start moving. I look back at the two girls, and they are going up and down, and man, it's hard to stand up, then it lifts up, up, and slams us down. We are out of control, and it's a ways away to get to the other end of the room; it starts again and it likes a huge wave, and you have to ride it out. I yell to the girls try to hold on to something, but it's too late; one of the girls gets caught under a washer and it landed on her. She doesn't make it. I grab the other girl and throw her toward the exit of the room, and then I make my way to it, and just like that the room goes back the way it was when we first saw it. The other girl screams out; she's so mad, she wants to go and get her friend, but I told her, 'You step one foot in there and it's going back the way it was. Let's go. We only have two rooms left."

As we start toward the greeting room, it's small, but we take are time as we enter it. I notice the stuff is nailed down to the floor. I tell her get ready to hold on to something, and just like that the room tips over, and we look at what was the floor and it's a twenty-foot drop into a pit it flips two or three times and then stops. Just as she goes to let go, I yell, "Hold on, it's a trick," and sure enough, it starts moving again, and she get flipped up, but luckily, she grabs a hold of a coffee table, then it goes back to normal. After a while we let go and escaped out of the room, and now the last room, and we will have beaten this place, but I knew it was the hardest one. The parlor: to me, is the hardest one to pass. We enter the girl is like, "Let's go."

I told her this was the room that the ceiling comes down on you.

She said, "We are running out of time, let's go!" So, like a fool, I listened to her and took off as fast as I could run, and the ceiling was coming down, but I never looked back. Just as I made it to the end, I yell to her, "We made it, you were right, we just had to run!" I look back and she didn't make it, three feet from the end; the ceiling fell on her. I felt so sorry for her. I then knew that I had to find my way out and hope to make the time, which I had no clue what it was. As I am trying to navigate through the house, I fall down one of the holes in the floor, and it sets me back a bit. As I make my way up from the hole, I can see the ending in site but can't get there, it's too difficult, and I hear a siren go off, then all the lights came on I was like, "Noooooooo!" I worked so hard to try and leave, but I just couldn't get out. I finally make it out the front door, and no one is there. It is so disappointing not having my family be there. I sat down and was exhausted.

Finally someone came to me and said, "Here is what you won, $210." I stood up and told the guy, "That's it? I risk my life for $210 bucks? What about the other people in there?"

He said, "That's why they signed a waiver, you knew the rules."

I was like, yeah, I did. I sat back down and couldn't believe this happened and I was involved in it.

The guy came over to me and said, "You made it out; that's an accomplishment, man." He then leans in and tells me, "You did a good job, you know. You weren't even supposed to make it out."

I look up at him and look over at the people coming out of the house that didn't make it and I feel a little bit lucky, but I know this will never end until someone finds a way to beat The House.

The End

The Picture

Judy and I were looking to buy a house as we had been together for four years, and it was time. We looked all around and finally found the house of our dreams, or so we initially thought. The agent had prior engagements, so when we scheduled a time to walk the property, he directed us to the mailbox where the key would be waiting. We arrived, grabbed the keys out of the mailbox, and approached the house. As we walked around the home, it had this weird feel to it, and it smelled funny in certain places. It was huge, though, but the more we walked around the more Judy had a bad feeling about the place. There were doors that we couldn't open and there were places that we didn't feel comfortable to go in. We left the house and decided to go to the realtor; we wanted some answers from him.

Once we got to the realtor's office, we asked him why he really didn't want to come to the house with us. We knew something was wrong and after walking through it proved our point.

"The house is haunted," he states with shaking hands.

I couldn't help but laugh. I knew Judy was serious about feeling weird and uncomfortable in the house, so I eased back on the laughter.

"No one is touching that house; it's been on the market for years. Whatever price you bid the place is yours," he spit out to us. I knew Judy would be mad if we didn't talk about that, so after a while of talking about it and convincing her it wasn't all that bad, she agreed that it would be a great purchase. We bought the house right on the spot, knowing we might change our minds if we dwelt on it for too long. We started cleaning and moving in hours later, going through things and throwing out old items left by the last owners. Judy noticed again that some of the rooms were locked, and we both realized no extra keys were given to us when we bought the place earlier.

"I think we should just tear it down and repair the door and frame later. What do you think?" I asked Judy. She agreed, with one swift kick to the locked door we stood in front of the opening.

We noticed the room was empty, and we weren't sure why it was locked in the first place. We then moved to the ballroom on the first floor to find the second door that was locked. We took some hammers to the door and finally for it opened; immediately, we felt a gust of wind that made our skin crawl.

"Damn, this room doesn't feel right," Judy said with a shiver. "I don't feel comfortable about this place."

"It's gone now, and if it comes back, I'm here to help you." I squeezed her shoulder to let her know everything was okay.

For a while we cleaned and threw out a lot of stuff. We moved on to remodeling and started painting and replacing the floor and walls. We went throughout the day with no problems, until we got settled in the kitchen for dinner. We had just sat down for dinner when the lights started to flicker. Before we knew it, the plates started to fly out of the cupboards, shattering on the floor. It was so unreal, then Judy started to scream, and I was in awe at what was going on. We grabbed what we could and headed outside. We could still hear the plates getting smashed and we could see the lights going on and off. It was a nightmare; we both couldn't believe our eyes. We got into our truck and headed into town; we couldn't stay there that night, so we got a hotel hoping tomorrow would be better.

The next day, we decided to visit the realtor again; we had to tell him about what had happened the previous night.

"Plates were flying, the lights were freaking us out. No more lies. You are going to tell us what happened there or you get the house back, it's as simple as that." I figured a threat would do the trick to get him to tell us what he was hiding about the house.

"Back in the late fifties, there was a young couple that were madly in love who lived in the house. One night, while the young man was working outside, he got shot by the neighbor. The neighbor was out hunting in the woods behind the house and hadn't realized how close he had gotten to their property and pulled the trigger on the first glimpse of movement he had seen . The young girl was devastated and ended up taking her own life in the house hours later; she couldn't live without him." We both nodded to the realtor, wanting him to tell us everything.

"After the house was fixed up in the seventies, it was sold to a drug dealer. People who were customers or neighbors remember him telling them he didn't like the house much, that he heard voices when he was alone, and things periodically moved places. Then, one night, authorities think while he was high, he managed to make his way to the third story, where he fell to his death. What is a mystery to all is how he even got up there; there is no access, no window to the third floor." By this point the realtor was avoiding our eyes, shaking his head as he looked at the floor.

"So, how can we fix our problem?" I urged.

"Well, this lady, she does voodoo and can tell you what you have to do to get your house back," he whispered to us and then pushed us a piece of paper with an address written on it.

We nodded in agreement and set out to see this lady, but we asked the realtor to come with us just in case.

The woman met us at the door of the address we had been given us.

"Oh boy, you two have a big problem." She then went into this trance as her eyes rolled in the back of her head.

"Can you help us?" I pleaded; we need your help.

"First, you have to change the house back. If not, they will find you and follow you everywhere," she directed. "Also, all the items you misplaced from the basement belonged to those who lived there first. You must put it all back," she warned.

I looked at Judy. "I haven't been in the basement, have you?"

"No, I haven't either," she said with her eyes wide.

"It must be one of the contractors," said our realtor. "You must retrieve that stuff that was in the basement, or they are coming for you two." We thanked the woman and hurried off into the night, knowing that we had a job to do tomorrow.

We woke up the next day and started to put the stuff back the way we found it. We fixed the doors upstairs and painted over the fresh paint with the old matching paint we found out on the porch. Then, after a couple of days, we were all done except for replacing that stuff that was in the basement, even though we had no idea who had it or what it even was. We finally got a hold of the realtor and asked him who had access to the basement.

"It's got to be one of the contractors. I can't remember who exactly, though," he apologized. We had hit a dead end, but we had to keep trying.

That night, driving back from one of the contractors' house, we started having issues with the car. The music was turning on and off, and so were the lights.

"KNOCK IT OFF," Judy screamed. "We did what you wanted. We put everything back the same way, what else do you want!"

Just then it got so cold in the car the windows fogged up. We start panicking until we noticed writing on the fogged-up glass that said, *YOU'RE MISSING SOMETHING*. We both screamed, slammed the car in park, and jumped out.

"We have to find that missing item, whatever it is; we need that!" I urged to Judy. "We need to go back and talk with the realtor. I think he's hiding something from us." We both agreed and waited a bit before getting back into the car and driving to the realtor's house.

As we pulled up to the house, we noticed that the realtor was wandering around outside with just his shorts on. I pulled into the driveway and ran over to see what was going on. It seemed as if he was in a trance, it's like a spell or something.

"Judy! Get me a glass of water," I yelled to her.

When she returned with the water, I threw it on his face, and he immediately woke up, startled and not knowing where he was or how he got there.

"I took this white clear picture of the house," he sobbed. "I didn't think it would be a problem, I just wanted it," he wailed as his shoulders shook up and down.

"You stupid bastard! That's why the house has come alive! It's because of you! That house is evil, and it wants that picture back; if not it's going to kill us one by one! Where is it?" I screamed at him, pulling his shoulders so he would look at me.

"It's in my basement. I don't want it anymore," he sobbed. We ran into the house and down to the basement, slowly walking over to the painting.

"It feels weird down here, Judy," I said, and just when I went to grab the picture, I felt an electric jolt sent me flying toward the ground.

"Holy shit! What happened?"

"I can't touch it; you try."

"That's nuts! I doubt it." She tried and went flying backwards just like I did.

"It looks like the only person to bring it back will be the person who took it."

Just then the picture began to show white, and it started to move.

"Judy, we have to get this picture back or we are in big trouble." We went up the stairs and to tell our realtor that he needed to be the one to return the picture.

"I am not touching that thing, especially if that is where this crazy stuff is coming from." He shivered as he spoke.

"You better! Judy and I can't grab it or touch it. It has to be you," we pleaded with him, hoping he would give in. After convincing him, he agreed to bring the picture back to the house, but we had to go with him. We were just feeling grateful that this all would be over soon enough.

We got to the house, and it just felt so weird and creepy. We went in, and it looked as if a tornado hit our home; furniture and everything near it had been swept up and spit out across the house.

"This house is alive." We looked at the realtor, hoping he would start to understand what we've been going through. I grabbed Judy's hand, and we walked behind him as we headed down the stairs to the basement.

"You must put it back right at the same spot you found it," I directed the realtor, making sure he knows.

He nodded in acknowledgement. As he was walking with the picture, the feeling of uneasiness started to fall upon us, and as he placed it on the hook, all of the lights turned off and immediately turned back on. I heard the realtor scream. Judy and I look over, and there are faces everywhere, staring right at him. I look between the realtor and the picture and started to understand.

"Look! It's the people from the picture," I stated, pointing to the frame hanging on the wall.

Just then the realtor screams again, "I can't let go of the picture," as his hands struggle to leave the frame hanging on the wall. Before we know what is happening, the group extends farther out of the picture, outstretched arms reach for the realtor as he is frozen in place. He is engulfed in dozens of hands that cling to him with one purpose. He is screaming and begging for help, but Judy and I were glued to the spot, and with a bright light and a crash of thunder, the realtor is gone and the picture lies face down on the floor.

Judy went over to pick it up the picture, and as she looks at it, she gasps and drops it, landing on the floor facing up. I slowly walked over to look at it and place my hand over my mouth and back away in awe. The people are now surrounding the realtor, who has been frozen in the picture with his mouth wide open, screaming for help.

We understood what had happened all those years; the house had captured people who tried to take the picture out. I picked the picture up and rehung it back in its original place. I grabbed Judy's hand and led her out of the house and into our truck.

"Let's start again, shall we?" I asked Judy.

"I wouldn't want it any other way," she responded as she squeezed my hand in return.

To this day we still haven't returned; we left our belongings with the hope of starting new. We still hear stories about the house from hundreds of miles away, but we sigh in relief. We know we escaped with our lives, but others haven't been so lucky.

The End

Three Wishes

A young boy named Brad is running one day on a bike path; he notices this shiny object in the tall grass. The sun just hit it the right way, and there it was. He moves the tall grass and finds out that it is very small, what looks like a genie lamp, and it looks like it has been there for a while. The grass had been growing around it; he couldn't pull it up, then he noticed what looked like rope around the base of it, but it was rotten and wasn't holding it tight enough, so he gave it a big tug, and it came free. He brought it home and began to clean it up, and to his surprise, the more he cleaned it the more it started to shake, and he couldn't hold it any longer; he saw smoke coming out of the spout. After a while, this man popped out of the lamp.

He was a tall, dark man with this outfit of what a genie would wear but older looking. He just floated in the air above the young boy who was in awe at the sight of the man. Just then the man says, "Young man, thank you for setting me free." I am your Genie, Shabbi. You now have three wishes. Use them wisely, my boy,: and just like that he starts to go back in the lamp just then the boy said, "Wait." The genie pops back up and says, "Yess?"

The young boy said, 'How will I find you?"

The genie laughs out loud; he says, 'Just call my name, SHABBI! I will be there." The boy nods and just like that the genie goes back into the lamp. So the young boy goes to school, thinking all day long what he wanted from the Genie, and once school was done he hurried home to get his lamp and tell the Genie what he wanted.

He runs home and goes right up to his room and there on his nightstand is the lamp. He says, "Shabbi," and out comes the Genie; this time he is dressed in all new clothes and looks all cleaned up. The boy then asked Shabbi, "How come you look so different?"

The genie told him that he has no powers or can't go anyway until someone releases him, "Which you did, and now your three wishes."

The boy still had no idea what he wanted; the genie then said, "A new bike maybe," and a new one appeared just like that, and the kid was like, "Nah."

Then the genie said, "What about a skateboard."

There was like, "No." Then he said, "Let me think about it."

The genie then said, "Hey, kid, you need to pick something. COME ON!!! I want to get out of here!"

The kid said, I'll tell you when I'm ready."

Just like that the Genie goes back in the bottle. He's pissed and comes up with an idea to switch places with the kid. "But how?" the Genie said to himself and then just like that he's got it.

Later that day the kid comes home, and the Genie appears and says to the kid, "Well, Mr. Brad, how was your day?"

The kid said it was ok, then the Genie said, "Are you ready for your wishes?"

Brad said, "Well I'm ready for one anyway," and the Genie said, "Okay, what is it? What would you like?"

"I want a new bike not just a bike, the fastest mountain bike ever made."

The Genie then waves his hands in the air and just like that a cloud of smoke and right in front of Brad is a Cannondale bright orange, big, knobby tires.

"The fastest mountain bike ever made," says Shabbi.

Brad is so pumped; he can't believe it and he rides it almost the whole evening; when he comes back, Shabbi starts in with his plan.

He starts with music and bright lights coming out of the lamp, and Brad picks it up and Shabbi tricks him into thinking it's unreal inside the lamp, so Brad calls him out and he says, "Yes...."

Brad said, "What's going on in there?"

"Oh, just a little party," Shabbi says, and he then says, "Would you like to join, Brad?"

He thinks about it for a bit and then says, "Nah, I'm tired. I'm going to bed." Shabbi then goes back in his lamp, pissed that he couldn't get him to go in. He thinks of another way, and he's got it.

"I know what to do."

The next day, Brad was up early and was out on his bike that afternoon. Shabbi puts his second plan into action. Just then Brad comes in and says, "Shabbi."

Out of the lamp he comes and Brad says, "I want this." he shows Shabbi a go-kart. with a wave of his hands and a puff of smoke Shabbi says your second wish Brad looks outside and there is his go-kart. Just as he leaves his room, Shabbi grows large and looks down at Brad. "Remember you only have one wish left, Brad!"

 Brad never said a word and he just went down and got on his go-kart.

That afternoon, Brad walked into his room, and he heard music coming out of the lamp and he called Shabbi and his voice came out of the lamp. "Yes, Brad, how can I help you?"

Brad was really curious; he said, "What's going on in there? It's sounds like fun." "It is," Shabbi said.

Brad then said "Can I go inside your lamp?"

"Sure you can, no problem," Shabbi said, and he said, I'll be out in a bit." As he comes out he said, "drink this, young man," and Brad had no clue what he drank, but the next thing he knows he is getting smaller, and soon he is getting sucked inside the spout of the lamp. As he heads in the lamp, he lands on this huge couch with a lot of pillows, and it's supposed to be music and bright lights. It's not, it's old and dirty and dusty, and where is Shabbi? Brad yells to him, and nothing; he's not around. "I can't seem to find him anywhere and I am stuck in here," Brad yells again and again, and finally, "he see him floating in the air." Brad says he wants out.

He said, "Oh no, you"re stuck in there we traded places."

I told him, "No, we didn't, plus I have one wish left have you had forgotten about that."

I tell him, "Shabbi, I want out of here," and he said, "Remember that's your last wish."

I said, "No, no, it's not. I take that back. My last wish is—"

Just as I was about to tell him my wish he leaves, and now what do I do? I was so mad!! I could scream!! I then hear this voice coming from what looked like the hallway and it's another kid a little older than I am, and he looks like he's been here for a while. I introduce myself, "Hi I'm Brad."

"Hi Brad, I'm Kevin," and we sit and he tells me stories of what Shabbi has done and how he tricks kids into getting them to switch with him. "Now you are trapped, Brad," Kevin said,

I said, "Oh, my friend, I still have one wish left and then next time he comes down we will get him."

Kevin said, "You have to say it in front of him, so your wish gets granted. After that please get us out of here."

I said, "How many are there?" and fifteen to twenty kids came out. I was in awe. I couldn't believe all these kids had been tricked by this guy. We have to get them out of here, so I told all the kids what we are going to do. "The next time he comes down here, we are going to get him. We will act like we are having a huge party, and once he comes in, we get him. I'll yell out want my wish is and once he gets me out, I'll get him for you guys."

So we put our plan into action. We get lights that the kids have we find some music and we dress up Shabbi's place, and it really looked great, so I told all the kids to put the plan in action. So we started with the lights and music, and I told the kids to dance around and get this going. As we started, it didn't take him long to come down and inspect what was going on, and he was like, "What's going on?" as he floated above all the kids, then he landed on the floor. Just as he did, the kids all gathered around him and grabbed him; now he couldn't escape or he would take everyone with him.

Just then he's struggling to get away; he then threatens the kids. Just like that they let go of him except me, and I was right behind him, and I whisper in his ear, "I wish for three more wishes."

He says, "NOOOOO."

Just then I wished myself out of the lamp, and I wished the kids out, then once I said that they all went back to where they came from, then I looked at him. He looked dejected, and I then said, "I wish you were inside the lamp and don't ever come out!"

He yells, nooooo. I just wanted to have some fun. Come on, Brad."

"Your fun is over Shabbi," as he goes into the lamp and a great feeling comes over me as all the stuff he got me disappears and everything is back to normal.

The next day, I walked out into the deepest part of the forest and dug a hole, and I did exactly what the next person did. I tie a rope around the bottom of the lamp and put it in the hole. "Enjoy yourself, Shabbi, you should never be let out."

As I am covering him up I hear him yelling, "I'll get you, Brad. Oh, this isn't over, you'll see," and I hear him laughing as I cover him up.

The End

Treachery

It was a warm summer day in the UK and I was working on the farm, plowing the fields to getting ready to plant, when the plow hit something; it was big enough to push the tractor a little sideways, and I had no idea what it was. As I went around and looked back, it's shiny and long. I was stunned at what it looked like. As I plowed around it, I see that it's huge and shiny, and the more I move the dirt, it looks like a wing of an airplane. I was in awe at this. I couldn't believe a plane was buried in our farm field all these years. I go up to the house and get Dad and bring him down to see . He's in his eighties and would know exactly what happened out here. As I explain what it is, he's also confused a little to have this on the property. See, he said that we just started planting over in that field just a couple years ago, and I was like, "Only the second or third person to plow over there," so he wasn't sure himself.

As we get there, he has this smile on his face. "Jesus," he says, "that sure looks like a planes wing." He told me to go up and get the big tractor with the bucket and dig it out. I was like, "You sure, Pops?"

He said, "Oh yeah, it has to come out."

So as we start digging, I realize that it's a German plane, and it's in real good shape. I then have a hole about twenty feet wide by twenty long and at least fifteen feet deep. I then hook up a strap on the underside of the plane and begin to pull it out of the hole. As we began to pull it out of the hole , I notice that there are still two pilots inside the plane, well there skeleton remains. That's when we called the Bobbies to come and see what we could do. As the Bobbies pulled in, they were at an awe also; they asked me how did I find this. I told them the whole story, and they couldn't believe it, either. We then finished burring the hole and brought out the generator and hooked it up to the pressure washer, and we washed the entire plane and then moved it to a drier place closer to the house. They then called the coroner, and he came over; we opened up the cockpit, and the two pilots were just skeletons, but we showed respect and took them out and bagged each one and was hoping that their families could get some closure. As for the plane, it was in unreal shape. I cleaned up the cockpit and charged the batteries to see if it would start and see if the engines would turn over, when I discovered something underneath after I accidently hit a lever inside the cockpit that stopped me in my tracks. It opened up the bottom boom doors, and there was this massive boom just hanging there, ready to go.... A BOMB! I was like *holy shit*. I then pushed that lever back in and it went back up and closed the door. Wow, that bomb is ready to go.

A couple of weeks went by and things were back at the norm at the farm until, one day, we get a call from this strange man asking if we are the people who found the plane. My dad answers and said yes. He asked if he could come over and look at it. He said sure.

He said, "I have a lot of questions for you, and I assume you have a lot for me."

A week went by and this man approached the farm, I noticed he had a badge on his car door that I had never seen before, and he had two other gentlemen with him. They looked like scientists. I was baffled about this, but whatever, I guess. As they introduced themselves, we could tell they were German, and they were very excited about seeing the plane. As they started to look over the plane, they saw my electrical cord and asked if I had powered up the batteries. I came up with a lie and said, "No, it's for the pressure washer." They then asked if I was going to sell it. I was like, "I'm not sure what we are going to do with it, it is an antique now."

Then one of the gentleman said, "You know, it's Germany's property."

I then said, "Well, hmm, it's on my property and has been here for thirty years, and the last time I looked, we're not in Germany. Good day, fellas."

As they are leaving, the one that made the comment, kept staring at me. I asked him if he had a problem; the others grabbed him and said, "No, we are fine. Thank you for letting us look at the plane."

As they are leaving, I took a picture of their license plate and started to look for that symbol that was on the side of the car. I've never seen that before, and my dad thought it looked like the Schutzstaffel. My dad remembers them from the war, and it was the SS that had that emblem. I then was thinking that we needed to get that bomb somewhere because it's pretty clear that's what they are looking for; they never even asked about the two men that were inside.

So that night, with some help, we took that huge bomb down and put a barrel in its place, and we carefully hid the bomb inside the hey barn and covered it up until we could get someone over here to look at it.

The next day, I drove into town, and I noticed that car again. This time there was a truck with it just sitting there. I was getting a little worried about what we uncovered here. I didn't want anything to happen to my family. I then went over and picked up my supplies, and as I was walking toward my truck, there is that car again. This time it's kind of blocking me in a little. I said, "Well, hello, gentlemen. How are you?"

Just like that their attitudes changed a lot, and that one guy said, "We need that plane how much for it?"

Just then the one who I talked to raised his hand, and the other guys stopped talking. He said, "You're a smart guy, just do the right thing and give us the plane."

I said, "Is there something on it that you guys are looking for?"

Just like that he pushed me against my truck and said, "Listen, we can do this the easy way."

Just then a cop car drove by and stopped and told them, "Move your car. You're blocking people," then he noticed me and asked if anything was wrong.

I pushed back and said, "Nope, I'm good," got in my truck, and left.

As I got home, I went in the house, told Dad what had happened, and he said, "Son, you're best to just give them the plane." I told the hired hand to get all our guns, make sure we have everything set and we have ammo.

Dad then said, "Hey, we don't need to lose a life over a German plane."

I said, "No, we don't, but this is our property, our men died on this field, and I won't let them take it."

He then thought about it and said, "Okay, son. I get where you're coming from. He then asked, "What are you going to do?"

"I'll have a huge surprise for these guys when they come back."

He got on the phone with the British Armed Forces and let them know what was going on what we found, and I also told them about those guys what they want, he then said we will be down, and they sent two trucks. We hid them in the barn, and sure enough, here come those Germans again.

The Commander of the Brits said, "Don't do anything until they get out of the car and truck."

Just as the German leader came out and started yelling, "You know what we're here for. Come, get out of there." The commander then gave the word, and the Brits surrounded the Germans and said, "Hey, boys. You best put your guns down; if not, you won't make it home."

The leader then said, "You don't know what you're doing."

The commander said, "What branch are you from?" He didn't answer. We can check, now boys arrest them.

Just then their leader said, "We are with the Independent Germany."

Then my old man said, "You mean the SS."

He smiles. "You remember us, old man."

My dad then said, "Oh, I do, and I've killed a lot of you bastards."

The guy went to lunge at my dad, and I put my pistol in his face and said, "That would be a big mistake."

The commander then said, "Let's call the German Military and see if they want this plane and its inhabitants."

As he gets off the phone, he then says to me, "This plane was a special secret plane to go behind enemy lines and drop that bomb. By the way, it's filled with highly toxic killing chemicals, so handle that with care."

I was like, "Holy shit, yup, we want that gone." The Brits then escorted the German men off the property. We then watched the military guys take that away, and then they came for the plane. I was a little upset that they took the plane but understood what had to happen.

A couple of weeks go by, and Dad and I are out on the field where the plane was. We were just finishing fixing the grounds when the commander came over and handed us each two envelopes. Dad opened his up first and said, "Oh my." He had to sit; it was a flying cross medal. I also had one, with a letter that said, "Thanks to you guys a lot of lives were saved because the love of your country. England appreciates your dedication, and loyalty and please wear those medals with pride." Your Queen Elizabeth!

Just then we see a plane coming back, but it's not the German plane, it's our own Spitfire, and the commander said, "Where would you boys want this?"

Dad was smiling from ear to ear.

"Since you lost the first plane, the Admiral gave you one of our own." Dad wanted it over behind the big tree in front, so when you drove by the highway, you could see it and hope that it gives everyone the feeling of Patriotism.

The End

Johnny D Hypnotist Magician

The first time I met Johnny D was when my cousins and some of my friends wanted to quit smoking, so they saw this ad about this hypnotist who would hypnotize you and make you stop smoking, so I went with them to see if this really works. So, as they went in, I went to some other show downtown, and I told them I would meet up after, so they went. When we met up later, I was curious to see if it worked. Two were already smoking, and one said he smokes more now. As I start to laugh, one girl in the group said, "I really have no urge to smoke."

So we all said, "Well there, Johnny D, he's the man, one out of ten." We all start laughing and then we head over for dinner. After dinner, most of us go home and head to bed, and some stay downtown and have a couple drinks at the bar, and as the night goes on, from the bar, we see a couple of the people in our group walking outside and we yell to them, "Hey! Where are you guys going?" But nothing, no response from them, and we were like, "What's going on?"

As we head outside, they are gone; where did they go? It's the strangest thing. It's not like those guys to just run off like that. Something's happening, and we need to see what's up. We split up and start looking for them, but we were unsuccessful, and we start heading back to the hotel, when we then hear an alarm going off, and we look at each other and can't figure it out where it's coming from, and just like that, a couple blocks away, we see one of the guys walking toward the hotel, and we yell at him, but he never stops, just keeps walking, and by the time we get to where he's heading, nothing; he's gone.

I was like, "This seems strange. What's going on here?"

We were like, "Whatever, man," so we go back in and really don't think about it much until day two of this weekend when I can't sleep one night, and I look out the balcony and I see the same guy with two girls now walking like they are zombies, heading downtown? What is going on here?

I get dressed and head downstairs and try not to get caught by anyone. I am going to find out what's going on here. As I head outside, I come across one of the ladies, just standing there. I look at her, but she is OUT. It looks like she is sleepwalking, or she is under a spell, and farther down the street I see another girl, just standing there also, so I sneak around the first one and head toward the second girl, and I look around, and she's near the end of the street, just standing there. Right across the street, I see that guy again. He's right in from of this expensive store they sell clothes, jewelry, etc., a very nice store, and all of a sudden, he throws a huge rock through the front glass and walks right in. The alarm is going off, and I yell, "Man, what are you doing!"

But no response from any of them, and he comes out really fast with a bag of stuff, and just like that, they head back to what looks like the hotel, and I am following them this time, staying way back so they don't see me. As they get to what looks like the back entrance, I duck down. I step on a piece of wood that slams into a metal trash can and makes a huge noise. Just like that, I look over, and they all turn their heads and start walking toward me. I am about to run away, when a cat jumps out of the back of the corner and heads away from my spot, and they stop and walk back towards the rear of the hotel. The garage door opens, and in they go.

I am like, "Something fishy is going on here."

I then go into the hotel and go and wake up my friends. I tell them the whole story. They are like, "What do you think is going on?"

"I don't know, but we are going to find out tonight. That's two burglaries in two days, and I think I know who's doing this."

They are like, "You do?"

"Oh yes, and I am going to show you guys tonight."

So we set up a plan to see who's behind this, and we put it into action. I sent the two girls down near the strip just to hang out until they hear from us.

"What are we doing?" my friend ask me as we head down to the end of the street near the jewelry store.

I tell him, "We are waiting because this will be day three of the burglaries and it's like clockwork." So as we wait for what feels like forever, we see the same three, the two girls and one guy, walking from the hotel storage garage and heading back to the strip but walking like they have no clue, and I show my buddy, "Look at their faces."

He's like, "Their eyes are closed!"

I was like, "Yes, like they are hypnotized."

He then says, "Holy shit! Johnny D."

"YES, YES!" I say, "It took me a couple days to figure it out. Okay, let's see where they are going today." As we follow them down the back doors of the rear building, it's different this time. Before, they were checking the doors to see if they were unlocked. Now it looks like they are going to a specific place. It's a small credit union on the rear of the strip. I was like, "We need to see if we can wake them up somehow, but how?" I wasn't going to get caught, because you don't know what they would do to you.

I told him, "I got an Idea. Let's go back to the hotel and find where Johnny is. Maybe if we figure out what he's doing to hypnotize the guys, we could stop him."

So we both head back to the hotel and try to find where he is. We look up on the floors, but no one around. We then head to the basement, and we hear this whistling noise. We then head toward it, thinking that this is what he's controlling them with, but instead, it is this box that he is scratching that is making this weird noise. We see him sitting near the window and he scratches it every five minutes. We then see him leave the area. We then head over, grab the box, and head out and head upstairs and over to the strip. We hear him yelling, and we start running faster until we run into the guys that were hypnotized.

They are like, "Why are we down here? What's going on?"

We explain the whole thing to them, and they are pissed, so we come up with this plan to pretend that they are still hypnotized, and we then will get him at his own game. As he rounds the side of the strip's first building the guys that have been hypnotized just stand there. He is like, "No, no, no, come on. This can't be happening." He then tries to make them move, but they don't move. He starts to panic, and then claps his hands, and they start working their way back to the hotel, but instead of going to the hotel they walk right buy and are heading to the police station down on the end of the block. He's yelling to them but to no avail, they just keep moving.

Meanwhile, we were at the police station telling them what he did, and they come out and surround him, and he says, "Well, hello, officers. How can I help you?"

They say, "What's going on here?"

He then says, "Well, I think the kids accidently got hypnotized at my show. My name is Johnny D., The Hypnotist."

The officers then turned and said to the kids, "are you guys hypnotized" and they all opened up their eyes and turned to Johnny D. and said, "NO!! He hypnotized us to steal money and jewelry for his benefit."

Johnny then said, "No, no, I didn't do that," and just like that the cops arrested Johnny D and took him in. The officers went to his room and found all kind of money and jewelry. They think he has been doing this for years. He would pick people out of the audience who could be easily hypnotized, and he would use this box to get them up in the night and control them with it. We are so happy that we took this guy off the streets, so he doesn't trick anyone else into stealing. After that, we all went back into the hotel to sleep. It's been a long weekend, we all agreed, a weekend to remember.

The End

Wrong Place, Wrong Time

I guess this had to be the worst day in our lives, the day we saw this man die. See, my buddy Craig and I were heading downtown to get something to eat, and he needed to look at this apartment he was going to buy when this all went down. See, we notice this guy on the roof of the other building across from us, he was yelling. At the time, we thought it was at his buddy, but it wasn't. You see, the argument went from the roof to what looked like their room, and then we saw pushing and shoving. We noticed this through our room directly across from theirs. I tell Craig, "Look at those two."

Just then, we take our eyes off the rustle, and we hear a gunshot! We both looked over there, and sure enough, that one guy who was yelling shot the other. We both look at each other and are like, "Holy shit!"

Just then, the guy looks over, and we both hit the floor as quick as we could. He then yells over, "I see you two, and you're next."

I was like, "We need to get out of here." We make it to the door, and we start heading out, and we call 911 and let them know what we saw and what the guy said.

We then make it to the end of the hallway where there is a window, so we look over to see if the guy has left yet, and he notices us again. He's going down the same way we are in the opposite side. I start panicking and say, "Craig, we have to move to the rear of the building. He thinks we are coming out the front." So we started to head to the rear and take the back elevator to the loading docks so we could get out of there.

Just as we hit the door and start walking to the car, we notice this guy way away from us. He yells, and we hear two or three shots. We start running and make it to the car; just as we speed away, we see the cops go flying by us, and we slow down to see what is going to happen, and we see that guy walk right by the street, and he got off Scott free. No one notices him, no one seen him except us. He then notices us and starts running.. I tell Craig, "We got to go!" He then slams the gas pedal, and we head out and make a hard right turn at the light down the road, and there is a checkpoint. Two officers then yell at us to slow down! They approach the car, and Craig tells the officers the whole story. They have us drive through and park the car and wait there.

We then meet the detective that questioned us, and we tell him the whole story as well, and he said, "You boys might want to get out of town until we find this guy."

"Are we going to get protection, Detective?"

He said, "Does he know you two?"

We say, "No, we've never seen him before."

So the detective said, "You know how many people are in the city? You'll be fine, just stay low key." He gives us his card. "If you need anything or the guy tries something, call me." So we headed out over to Craig's apartment. It was more in the city than mine, and we both thought it would be better to stay at his place.

So, the day goes on, and we watch the news, and nothing. No one knows anything. Just then Craig's phone rings, and it's that guy. He said, "I don't know where you live. I don't know who you are, but I'm going to get you and your friend, Craig," then hung up the phone.

I was like, "We have to call the detective."

Craig then called the detective and then he said, "He contacted us. What should we do?"

The detective then said, "I'm sending over a car to watch you guys. Don't go anywhere. Stay in your apartment." Just when Craig got off the phone, we hear like, yelling coming from the stairs outside in the hallway of our apartment. We look at each other and start to panic a little, then Craig said, "Out the window."

We then hear someone pounding on the door. "I found you guys, hahahahaha."

We are like, "Shit, let's go," and we head out down the outside stairs to the ground. We look up, just as we see this guy in our apartment, and he then starts to follow us. We take off, and he heads towards the city.

As we get into the city, which is just down the block, it just so happens they are having some protest walk, so we get right in the middle of the protesters and just start yelling with them, and we are looking in the back of us, and a couple of people say, "What's wrong with you two?" We explain that this guy is chasing us, so just as we go to tell them about our story, this guy motions to two HUGE men, and boy, they are HUGE.

He says, "This guy is chasing our friend. Let's make it known we don't like it." Just then, Craig and I realize we are in an gay rights protest I told Craig I don't care. We look at each other and are so relieved. Just then we notice that guy is getting manhandled by those two big boys. We are so relived and laugh after, then Craig's phone rings; it's the detective.

"Where are you guys?"

We tell him what happed he said I'll send some men down to see if he is still there; he then told us to go to the nearest police station and stay there, he would be right over. We were so relieved.

We get there and tell the attendant what's going on and he tells us to just wait for him, so we are like, trying to process things in our head, trying to place the guy's face to anyone. Ugh, we just can't. It's so frustrating.

Just as we are relaxed, the detective walks in and goes right to the attendant, shows his badge, and says to us, "Let's go, boys. I'm going to take you to a safe house."

We were like, "Can't we get some of our things."

He said, "Nope, it's not safe there. He knows where you live."

Craig then says, "How does he know where we live? I just can't understand that."

The detective said he doesn't know either, so this house where is it, it's just on the outskirts of town. Oh, we were relieved. Just then, we drive out of the city. We get to this big white house with blue shutters.

He said, "We are here, boys. Let's get you guys settled in." As he goes to his trunk, he tells us to go in, it's unlocked, get settled in.

"Oh, okay."

So we head in and are thinking about how long we will be here. As we enter, we walk in and go to what looked like the living room and there was someone sitting on the sofa. I remember that person; it's the guy that has been chasing us.

I go to run, and there is the detective standing there, right in front of us, with his handgun drawn. I then turn to Craig, and I don't remember anything else.

We wake up with our heads hurting. The guy knocked us out and has us tied up back to back. We are gagged and can't move.

I was thinking about how to get out of here, but my head hurt so bad. I could feel the blood running down my face, then I blacked out again. I wake up this time, and it's night out, and I try to wake up Craig. We don't have the gags on anymore but now no one is around. The place is pitch black.

Craig finally wakes up, and he is in pain like I was. I told him, "It's going to take a bit for you to come around." As he gets his bearings, I'm trying to think of a way out of here. The only light in the house is through the moon outside, and it's not so bright.

I tell Craig, "Are your feet tied?"

He said, "No, just my hands, and chest too."

I told him, "Let's see if we can stand, and then we are going to drop right on the chairs. They are wooden, and hopefully, they break and get us out of here."

Craig was like, "I can't. My head hurts so much."

I told him, "If you don't do this, we are dead, you know it. We at least have to try."

After a bit of convincing, he said, "Okay, let's try."

We make it to our feet. I told him, "On the count of three, we jump up and land down hard on your seat."

"Okay," he said.

"One, two, three!" We hit the seat, and nothing. I hit so hard it jarred my teeth.

Craig said, "My god, that hurt my head so much."

I was like, "Well, that didn't work." Next, as I contemplated thoughts in my head on how to get out of here. I then had this other idea of trying to run and slam ourselves against a wall.

Craig was like, "Are you nuts? I can't take that, man."

I screamed at him. "DO YOU KNOW WHEN THEY GET BACK WE'RE DEAD!!! DEAD!!! Do you understand that, man! Come on, we have to try everything."

So we stood up, trying to remember where the wall was, and we took off, heading right for what we thought was the wall, but we hit whatever it was, went through that and landed in another room. Craig was on top. I was on the bottom on what felt like ice; it was slippery because of the blood coming out of my head, then I reached down and grabbed a piece of glass. I told Craig, "I have a piece of glass."

He yelled out a "God bless you for saving us."

I started to cut through the rope, and after what felt like an hour, I was through and untired myself and Craig.

As we sit up and go outside to see if we can find somewhere to go, we see an old barn in back of the house and what looks like a car in there. We hurry up as fast as we can, and the doors are locked, but I grab a rock and break one to get in. The inside lights come on when we open the door. we just need to try and start this up and get out of here. Craig tells me he knows how to do this. I was like, "What?"

He said, "Yes, I used to do this on the old truck at my grandfather's farm. Let me see." So he pulls some wires down and yanks some out and starts touching them together, and *bam*, the engine starts up. We get in and run right through the barn door and start out of trying to go somewhere. We find the main road, and we start heading anyway. We see a sign that tells us the city is twenty-five miles away.

I looked at Craig and he said, "We have a quarter tank of gas; try to cruise as much as possible, and don't speed. We don't need anyone pulling us over." So we stay on the road, going the speed limit, and we make it to the city. We get to the outskirts, and we head over to one of Craig's buddies' house, which was an old junkyard.

As we pull in, Craig hides the car and tells his buddy all about what was going on. He then said, "Watch this?" He goes over with this huge magnet and picks up the car by the roof and drops it in the cruiser. He said, "They are never going find out where you are." He then set up in the middle of the junkyard an old bus that was made into a camper inside. He said, "Stay here for as long as you want. I'll lock up, and you have the dogs to protect you." He then said, "Make a call to a different police department with this disposal phone, then throw it in the tractor trailer that's leaving today for California." We all laughed. Craig's buddy was cool Jesus it sounded like he did this before hahaha, and for the first time, we could relax for a bit.

The next day, Craig called the State Police and did exactly what his buddy said, and sure enough, the state boys were waiting outside the salvage yard, but we didn't open the gate until we knew the officers were alone and we could trust them. They came in, and Craig and I told them the whole story. The officers couldn't believe it but knew we were telling the truth, so this is what they were going to do, they said, "Call them and tell them you don't know what to do and you need their help."

We were smiling because we knew they were going to get what they desire. So, the State Police set up a bunch of officers in and around the salvage yard and put us right in the middle of it. Once they got in, he looked at Craig's buddy and told him, "Shut the gate and put your big loader in front of it."

We have all the other entrances blocked, we will get them; he then told us, "Try and get them to confess, then we will grab them." It seemed all good until the officers told me, "They may want to kill you right off," so he gave us a bulletproof vest to wear, then I became nervous. But I knew we need to get these guys, so Craig called. He then looked at me and said, "Here we go."

So the detective answered and said, "Craig, is that you?"

Craig was brilliant; he sounded scared. He then said, "Detective, we got nervous and got out of there, took the car in the barn, and now we are at a salvage yard in the city."

He then said, "Are you two okay?"

I said over Craig's voice, "Come get us out of here. This place sucks. It so dark."

Craig then said, "Quite." We both heard the detective sort of laugh. He then said, "You guys are in a lot of trouble."

We said we were sorry for leaving, just come and get us out of here.

He asked if we were alone. We both said yes. He then said, "Stay put. We will be there in twenty minutes, okay?"

"Okay, thanks," and we hung up.

The State cops told everyone to get into positions, we are live in twenty. Everyone took their places. I looked at Craig and told him, "Here we go, pal."

As they pull in, they are going really slow, and we see them from a distance, and we wave. They then get a little closer, and just then the detective stops and puts his window down and yells something out. We both look at each other. We yell, "We can't hear you."

He then turns his car to the side, and we see his face. He then says, "Get in the car. We will leave together."

Out of the corner of my eye I see the State guy motioning his hands no. I then say, "We have some questions for you."

He said, "Like what?"

"Why did you tie us up? Also, why did you hit us? I thought that was a safe house."

Just then he pulled his handgun out and said, "Just get in the car."

We move back into the dark. He then starts to come for us. I then hear, "Go, go, go!" The gate closes, and the huge loader blocks the door then the State boys all come out, guns drawn, and the detective is heading right for us, plus he's shooting at us, but it doesn't last long. The State boys return the fire, and he then drives his car into some junk cars over away from us. They go over, and that's it it's done. They shot him dead, him and his partner. We are so relieved that this is finally over.

"What a week," I told Craig.

He agrees with the State Police, then brings us home, and I look at Craig and tell him, "Next time you want me to look at a building with you, I'm not going."

He looks at me, and we both laugh.

The End